Cock of the Walk (Large Print)

By Wendy Laing

Writers Exchange E-Publishing
http://www.writers-exchange.com

Cock of the Walk
Copyright 2006, 2015 Wendy Laing
Writers Exchange E-Publishing
PO Box 372
ATHERTON QLD 4883

Published by Writers Exchange E-Publishing
http://www.writers-exchange.com

ISBN **ebook**: 9781921314506
Print: 9781921314025 (Amazon Assigned)

Cover Artist: Laura Shinn

* The dominant bully or master spirit. The place where barn-door fowls are fed is called "the walk". If there is more than one cock, they will fight for supremacy of this domain.

*Ref: Brewer, E, 1978, The Dictionary of Phrase and Fable,
Avenal Books, New York.

PROLOGUE
Cock-Crow Time

1

He fought for breath, choking, his heart pounding, clammy mist swirled around him. He peered through the steam and saw hot, bubbling water. Out of the foam, a large, wet, pink blob with wide, staring eyes bounced up at him.

No!

Joe Wilson lay in his bed, breathing heavily, shaken by the nightmare that had woken him so violently. The dream's vivid images still danced before his eyes in the dark. He took a deep breath and his heartbeat slowed down to its normal rhythm.

He forced a smile to his face, then shivered and stretched. "Come on, you idiot, it's only a nightmare. Snap out of it."

It was cock-crow time. The deep blue-black velvet cloak of the night sky was beginning to disappear as dawn approached. There was total silence. Even the frogs in the creek at the bottom of the hill were quiet. It was even too early for the morning chirps of the birds that would later scrounge for worms and other tasty morsels for their young.

Joe's mind began to wander quietly through the list of things that he needed to do that day. Check the vineyards, talk to the boss--Sir Peter--about the wine stocks, and also catch up with the work-experience boy from the local high school.

As the manager of Woodburne Wine Estate, Joe lived in the cottage at the foot of the hill. Sir Peter Percival's grandfather George Percival had built the manager's cottage and the mansion Woodburne, which squatted on top of the hill, overlooking the vines that grew on the estate. This imposing estate dominated the local township of Sunbury nestled at the foot of this hill.

Joe stretched again and turned over onto his side to look at the clock. It was almost six. He cancelled the alarm just a few seconds before it was due to ring, then got up and turned on the radio at a high volume so he could hear it from the bathroom as he showered.

Despite the warmth of the shower, as the steam fogged up the glass cubicle, a cold shiver tore down Joe's spine. Vivid images of the dream seemed to appear in the steam. He hurriedly turned off the water, stepped outside the cubicle into the cool air of the bathroom, dried himself, and then returned to the bedroom to get dressed. Sooty, his black cat, purred around his feet asking for some food.

* * *

At the same time Joe was dressing, there was movement in the chicken shed at the end of the home paddock. The big cockerel instinctively stretched and flapped his wings. He strutted out through the flap-door and hopped onto a low branch of the gum tree that stood inside the farm's fowl run, or walk. He was a magnificent creature, with black plumage that glistened with a bluish tinge when the streaks of the approaching light of dawn shimmered on them. The cock puffed out his chest and feathers, stretched up his neck, and opened his beak as wide as he could.

"Cock-a-doodle-dooooooooo!" he shrieked, then strutted around looking very pleased with the loud noise that he had just made.

The eastern sky was streaked with the orange glow of scattered clouds. It was nearly time for the sun to light up the countryside. As if in response to the cocks heralding, the sun crept up from behind the distant hills. A new day had begun at Sir Peter Percival's farm, Woodburne.

BOOK ONE
Birds of a feather

2

One of Detective Inspector Andy McNab's dogs nudged his hand. Andy yawned, looked at his watch, and muttered, "All right, Snow, I know it's time to get up."

More movement indicated that White, Andy's other poodle, had woken. Andy stretched his long legs, rolled to the side of the bed and got up to let the dogs out for their run.

Andy led a fairly solitary life. Most of his waking hours were spent dedicated to his police work. Any spare moment was carefully spent enjoying the solitude of the local countryside where his home was built on a ten-acre property. He had bought the property for his new bride Rhonda. However, the reality was that Rhonda had never lived at the farm as not long after their wedding, Rhonda became chronically tired. A visit to her doctor, and subsequent blood tests, confirmed an aggressive form of cancer.

Andy felt that he was now too selfish to be able to cope with someone else living with him permanently. He had thought about it of course, but he liked the fact that he did not have to clean the dishes if he didn't want to, or make his bed before rushing out of the door. In fact, he could easily produce dozens of reasons for living alone with only his dogs for company.

He was, however, a healthy active male with sexual desires. Any relationships were only with females outside the police force. He had no desire to get involved with a work-mate. Too many of his friends had succumbed to office relationships, which seemed to inevitably end up in a tangled mess with both parties retreating like injured dogs to lick their wounds. He had no intention of being wounded by love again.

Andy quickly showered, dressed and grabbed a quick breakfast. He took a brisk walk around the home paddock with the dogs following in his shadow. After the walk, he got into his car for the hour drive south to the city of Melbourne.

As his car cruised down the motorway, his thoughts turned to what the new day might have in store for him.

Joe carefully maneuvered the four-wheel drive truck around the rows of vines, whilst observing the local wildlife. Energetic birds rushed about their daily, dawn tasks of finding worms for little baby chicks nestled in the nearby gums that bordered the northern paddock.

Joe smiled at the young adult magpies, still begging for food from their stressed parents who were constantly dashing back and forth looking for tasty morsels of underground food to carry to the magpie teenagers and promptly shunt down the open beaks. The young birds almost choked with the food, but each time they bounced up squawking for more.

It was during these morning inspection tours around the Woodburne estate, that Joe fully related to the saying of "being at one with the earth." He loved his job and hoped that he could stay at Woodburne forever. These moments of contemplation and reflection always made him feel good at the end of the drive.

He turned the truck around the last vine-covered paddock and headed back towards the homestead. The sun was well up into the sky now, and, as the land began to warm up after the cool night, steam rose, creating an almost eerie look, like a medieval landscape. With a little imagination, one could envision a knight in shining armour riding over the top of the hill. As if on cue, a horseman appeared, startling Joe out of his reverie.

He waved and Jason, Sir Peter's son, waved back, before turning his horse and cantering over the hill, heading down towards the creek at the back of the property.

Joe drove to the foot of the hill, then opened and passed through the paddock gate. A cold shiver shot through him as he closed the gate. He shrugged his shoulders, got back into the truck, and drove up the driveway that wound up the hill towards the imposing house that dominated the top.

Woodburne was a blue stone, two-story, rambling house, with the traditional colonial verandas surrounding the lower and upper levels. The verandas were very elegant, with fine wrought iron framing each section. At the centre of the second level, a tower emerged. The tower enclosed a spiral staircase that led to a small balcony situated just beneath the dome. There was a magnificent view of the valley and the town of Sunbury from this lookout.

When Sir Peter Percival was in residence, the housekeeper Joan Rogers, made sure that the Australian flag was hoisted up the pole on top of the tower during the daylight hours. She was a proud believer in her colonial heritage. At the same time, she was quietly amused by the fact that the locals seemed to regard Sir Peter as almost local royalty.

Joe parked the car, then went through the gate into the side garden, his shoes crunching the fine shale chips on the footpath.

The gate at the end of the formal garden opened into the secluded, private garden surrounded by a high hedge and fence. Elm, oak and ash trees were scattered about a large, manicured lawn, while at the eastern edge of the garden there was a pool and enclosed spa. Sir Peter habitually used both every evening before retiring to bed. Joe frowned, watching steam hiss and spurt from underneath the spa door.

"Why on earth is the boss using the spa at this hour? He never uses it in the morning." Joe opened the spa room door, then gasped as hot, chlorinated steam billowed out at him. Lungs screaming for air, heart pounding, he pressed the "off" button at the edge of the spa, and waited for the steam to clear. When it did, he drew back in horror. A pink, wet body floated in the tub, eyes staring blankly his way. He stumbled backward, fell to his knees and retched.

When he recovered, he scrambled to his feet and half ran, half stumbled through the back door of Woodburne. He picked up the phone in the kitchen and with trembling fingers dialed 000. As he waited to be connected one word dominated his thoughts.

Dead! Sir Peter's dead.

3

"'Morning, sir."

Detective Inspector Andy McNab returned the greeting with a genuine, warm smile. His piercing blue eyes cast a quick look of approval at the woman who had made the greeting

"'Morning, Sarah. Another day, another murder?" he asked.

"You'll regret you said that," the Detective Sergeant replied.

"A suspicious death has been reported to us; ten minutes ago from Sergeant Dennis Sinclair of the Sunbury Police Station."

"Sunbury? That's a job for the locals, surely!"

"Sergeant Sinclair has asked us to go and investigate this one, sir. The deceased is Sir Peter Percival."

Andy started. *What? Sir Peter? Dead? Damn.* He took a deep breath.

"Sir Peter Percival? I drove past Sunbury only forty-odd minutes ago." He sighed. "Go ahead, lass, tell me the story so far."

"According to Sergeant Sinclair, According to

Sergeant Sinclair, Sir Peter was found dead this morning at seven-thirty. He was in the spa, which was superheated, and had been dead for several hours. The local doctor's first impression is that he died of a possible heart attack. However, Sergeant Sinclair and the doctor want us to go and check the area before the body is moved to the morgue for an autopsy." Sarah paused a moment. "Sergeant Sinclair knows that there have been recent allegations of corruption within the local farmer Co-op, and that Sir Peter Percival, as the local Member of Parliament, had asked for your unofficial advice about these allegations. Sinclair also realizes the possible implications of Sir Peter's death."

"Implications? That's a lovely generalization. Thanks, Sarah. Looks like we're going to Sunbury. Ask Detective Constable Ng to grab his gear. This will be a good case for him to cut his teeth on, eh?" Andy grinned.

Sarah smiled back. "There's time for a quick coffee. I'll get your usual de-caf and, while I'm out, I'll tell Vincent the news. He's been waiting for the last week for a murder investigation."

"Careful, Sarah, it's not officially murder--yet. I need to make some calls before we go to Sunbury, so the coffee will go down well, lass. Besides Sir Peter won't be going anywhere."

"Yes, boss. I won't mention the M word to

Vincent yet. He's going to be too keen on the job as it is." She slipped out of Andy's office. Andy sighed and leaned back in his office chair, his thoughts in a whirl.

Sir Peter was dead? It was only two days ago that they had dined together at Woodburne, talking about the Co-op's missing funds. The books showed an average amount of funds had been deposited and accounted for, whilst members said substantially larger funds had been originally collected. The question was--what had happened to those extra funds? Had Peter been getting too close to the answer? Had he, indeed, been murdered?

Andy looked up at Sarah as she returned with the coffee.

"Are you all right?" she asked, handing him the mug.

"I only saw Sir Peter two days ago. It's going to be awkward investigating the death of someone I know. Not that I knew him intimately, but we'd chatted on a few times." He stroked his moustache with his right index finger.

"Vincent is on his starting blocks, ready to go," Sarah said. "I'll get ready myself. Won't be long."

Although he watched her leave, Andy was again deep in thought. If it was murder, it would cause a rumbling like an earthquake through Parliament. Sir Peter was the Premier's golden boy. Andy sighed, made two quick phone calls, then sipped his hot coffee. He smiled after the second call. Good, Sir John Grey was available and ready to go to the death scene. Andy had great respect for Sir John. He was one of the most capable Forensic Pathologists in the country. Grey lived near to Sunbury and was still at his home in Romsey, which meant he would arrive at the scene before they did.

Sarah returned with her satchel-style handbag over her left shoulder. "Are you ready to go, sir? Vincent is rearing to go and I'm ready when you are."

"As you asked so nicely, yes, let's go."

4

The three detectives sat in silence as the police car purred northwards along the toll-way, Detective Vincent Ng driving. His face reflected deep concentration on his task, as the road was busy with the early morning rush of traffic.

Gradually, the suburbs started to disappear behind them as the toll-way took them closer to the zone where the Melbourne International Airport was situated. Ng stayed on the Calder highway that led to the city of Bendigo in the north. The turn-off that would take them over the main highway to the right into Sunbury was about fifteen kilometers north of the airport

Andy was again deep in private thoughts. *If this is a murder case, it was going to be a difficult one. Not only was Sir Peter a Member of Parliament, but he was a highly influential and wealthy businessman. There could be possible suspects scattered all over the state of Victoria!*

He smiled as he remembered a remark that his only living relative back in Scotland had said about the 'Colony of Victoria' during his last visit.

"Victoria is small, Andy. You must miss

Scotland surely, lad. Don't you miss being a policeman on the beat in Edinburgh?"

He had carefully pointed out to his cousin that Britain's landmass fit into the State of Victoria. He had found it impossible at the time to explain why he loved his new job and adopted country. There were still moments of nostalgia for his native country of course, but he loved Australia deeply, too. Andy thought about the painstaking investigation that possibly awaited them if the autopsy revealed that Sir Peter's death was not accidental.

"What are the local police like at Sunbury, boss?" asked Sarah, her crisp voice breaking the silence.

Andy grunted, but didn't immediately answer.

Sarah grinned. "Hello, there. Are you with us or on another planet?"

"Oh, yes, I'm with you. I'm just beginning to realise how little I know about Sir Peter. Yet, we were supposedly friends in the business sense. Strange isn't it?" He sensed Sarah looking at him. "To answer your question, lass, the Sunbury police are a friendly lot. Sergeant Dennis Sinclair was born in Sunbury. I've known him for about six years. We first met not long after I'd married. Rhonda knew him and introduced me as her 'murderous' husband. Poor old Dennis nearly had a heart attack at the time. He's a good honest policeman, who's not frightened of bending the rules slightly to get to the truth. I've no doubt that his two new officers, Senior Constable Frank Collotti and Constable Julie Wiseman, will tread the same path as their boss. Dennis would insist on absolute loyalty from his squad at all times."

Absolute loyalty and honesty was just what Inspector McNab demanded of his own team.

"Are you separated from your wife or divorced?" asked Rhonda.

"Neither. Rhonda died of cancer five years ago. That's why I live alone."

Sarah blushed. "I'm sorry. I didn't mean to pry. It's really none of my business."

"There's no need to apologize, lass. I mentioned her first. I'm glad you both know about her now. I've been rather insular about her. I shouldn't be." He turned and looked thoughtfully at Sarah She was an intelligent lass, her nursing background was an asset and she was the best assistant he'd ever worked with. But he suddenly realized that Sarah kept her private life as separate from the force as he had kept his. He did know that she lived in a little unit near the city in Fitzroy. He also found out in general conversation that she liked to go bushwalking when off duty, and that they shared a common interest in classical music.

He shifted his gaze to their drive, Ng. A new recruit, Ng was an interesting character. Although a

Vietnamese refugee, he'd learned and mastered the difficult English language. He was dedicated enough to perhaps achieve his wish to be the first Asian-born Police Commissioner.

Vincent Ng turned off the highway and the police car headed towards the township nestled in the foothills ahead.

"Turn right at the second roundabout, then go straight ahead at the following roundabout. About one hundred meters down on the left-hand side, you will find the Sunbury Police Station," said Andy.

"Thank you, sir."

Andy's first impression of the town they approached was its neatness and quaintness. The second, and more in-depth, observation revealed a pleasant blending of an old settlement with the new establishment. Most of the modern additions to the original landscape didn't seem out of place. On the right hand side, the original wooden building of the country train station was still operational. But the station was nearly hidden from view by a new multi-storied car park and grocery store. A few hundred metres down the road there was a modern colonial style complex, which contained a hardware store, an electrical store and a video rental shop. Near the second roundabout where they turned right, was the local burger place, and a large petrol station with a twenty-four hour shop.

The car went over a narrow, bluestone bridge that passed over the railway line. Another roundabout lay ahead. As Andy McNab had stated, the Sunbury Police Station appeared on the left a little further down the street.

The Station was large and modern. Outside on the right hand side, however, was the beautifully preserved original timber courthouse complete with a rebuilt replica of the original bluestone gaol. The latter two buildings were being used by the local tourist authority as a base for the local information centre.

The three detectives paused for a moment in the warm summer sun, surveying the scene, then quietly, briefcases in hands, walked towards the front entrance.

5

A well-groomed Constable greeted them at reception. "Good Morning, sir. I'm Constable Julie Wiseman. Sergeant Sinclair is waiting for you."

"Good morning, Constable," replied McNab. ."May I introduce my team, Detective Sergeant Sarah Sedgewick and Detective Constable Vincent Ng. Has anyone from Forensic arrived yet? I've asked Forensic Pathologist Sir John Grey to come. He will be conducting the autopsy."

"Sergeant Robert Page from the Forensic Squad is already at the death scene with a police photographer. Sir John Grey is also attending with Sir Peter's local Doctor, Frank Poulter, sir," replied Julie, then added, "Please come this way. Sergeant Sinclair is waiting for you."

They followed her down the passageway to Sinclair's office. Julie Wiseman was everyone's image of a homely countrywoman. She was in her late thirty's and wore very little make-up, which enhanced her beautifully clear olive skin. The severe, short-cut, straight, brunette hair and the heavy fringe, however, did nothing for her underlying beauty. Just before Julie opened the office door, she turned to McNab.

"Sergeant Sinclair left Senior Constable Collotti at the scene to come here and take you there himself, sir." She then showed them into Sinclair's office.

Sergeant Dennis Sinclair was in his late forties. He was a big man with blonde hair that was thinning on top. His physique showed a rather tubby torso that bulged over his wide police uniform belt, and bounced up and down when he stalked around his office. He shook Andy McNab's hand vigorously. "Morning, sir. I'm glad you came so quickly. Hell of a way to start the day! I don't know why, but I tend to agree with Joe, Sir Peter's manager, that it could be murder. No evidence yet, of course. Doc Poulter feels the same. Although it looks like a heart attack on the surface, the doc reckons Sir Peter had a heart as strong as an ox. Sorry, I know I'm making assumptions. Too early yet, I know, mate."

The words had come out of his portly face in rapid succession, like a machine gun. He paused, took a deep breath, then looked at Sarah and Vincent and added, smiling, "G'day, you must be Detective Sergeant Sedgewick, and, of course, you're Detective Constable Ng. Andy has spoken highly of you both." He turned back to Andy. "I know you're anxious to inspect the scene as soon as possible. I'll drive ahead and guide you there now."

* * *

Fifteen minutes later, the two police cars arrived at the impressive wrought iron gates, hinged to large, blue-stone pillars that guarded the entrance to Woodburne. Near the entrance was the neat blue-stone cottage that lodged the Station Manager, Joe Wilson.

The cars wound their way along the vineyards, past an English-style duck pond on the left, then went slowly up the steep, winding track towards the top of the hill. At the top squatted the imposing mansion of Woodburne.

When the group had reached the heavy, oak front door, they turned briefly and looked back at the view. Sunbury lay before them like a beautifully etched Persian rug. It was like viewing the township from a low flying plane. Sir Peter's Place certainly dominates the local landscape, thought Andy.

The group went inside. It was beautifully cool and dark after the heat and glare outside. Sinclair led them through to the back of the large building and to the back door in the kitchen. The back door led to a veranda that overlooked the solar-heated, kidney-shaped swimming pool. To the right, the veranda had been enclosed. It was in this enclosure that the Spa Room was located.

Andy noticed Vincent Ng taking a deep breath

before he followed them, and walked towards the group of people next to the Spa room, ready to view his first possible murder victim.

6

A ndy looked at Vincent's pale face. The scene they all viewed was just as Joe has said in his statement describing his discovery of Sir Peter's body.

When the steam cleared, the first thing I saw was Sir Peter floating in the spa. It was horrible. His eyes seemed to stare at me, but looked dull and lifeless. I knew straight away that he was dead. My first thought was that he looked like a boiled pig!

Andy knew that Vincent had seen bodies as a child in Vietnam, lined up in the back of a truck outside an army tent that was a temporary morgue. To Andy, it was as though he was viewing the body through Joe's eyes. Andy McNab's articulate voice with the slight Scottish lilt echoed around the Spa room.

"As Sir John has indicated, on first observation it appears that Sir Peter may have died of natural causes; for example, a heart attack or some sort of respiratory failure. However, as he has stated, only an autopsy will discover the actual cause of death. I find it interesting that Sir John also notes that there appears to be evidence of some residue of froth around his mouth. The autopsy will clarify the cause of death as either a simple natural cause whilst taking a spa bath, or the result of a clever murder. What do you think, Sarah? Any comments, Vincent?"

"Well, boss, I have a feeling that this is not a normal death. I can't explain why, though," replied Sarah.

"I don't know what to think yet, sir," replied Vincent, blushing.

McNab looked at Vincent, smiled, then said quietly, "Don't worry, lad. This is only your first week in our squad. Keep observing, but for God's sake don't be too frightened to share your thoughts or feelings with us at any time. I promise that I won't laugh at any valid or sensible theory lad. Sarah will vouch for that, won't you?"

"The boss is right, Vincent. Just remember, we are a team and three brains are better than one," said Sarah.

Vincent smiled at McNab and Sedgewick. "Thank you, sir. I'll keep that in mind. Don't worry; if I have something to say that may help in any way, I'll say it. I really appreciate your advice, both of you."

Andy McNab smiled, too. He was glad that he

had recruited Vincent to his team. He always knew that Vincent had the potential to be an excellent detective, but was also glad that Sarah agreed.

McNab then turned and looked at Sinclair.

"Dennis, could you organise a detailed search of the garden? If this turns out to be murder we need to make sure that we haven't missed any vital clues at the scene."

"Consider it done, mate," replied Sinclair, who turned to Collotti and added, "Frank, get a search organized straight away."

Collotti, a squat, swarthy man, whose accent still reflected a slight Italian rhythm, nodded. "Yes, sir, right away."

McNab looked at Collotti as he walked over to two constables and started to wave his arms in various directions around the garden. We might need your knowledge of Italian, lad, when interviewing some of the local co-op farmers.

McNab turned away from Sinclair and the spa enclosure and faced the officials from the city morgue. They had been waiting patiently for the official authority to take the body away. Andy's voice boomed from the spa.

"Okay, lads. He's all yours now. You can take him away."

With those words, the body of Sir Peter Percival was carefully removed from the spa and put in a plastic body bag. The bag was zipped closed, placed on a stretcher, and carried to the mortuary van. Within five minutes, the van had disappeared down the winding driveway of Woodburne, taking its cargo, the late 'Cock of the Walk' to the city Morgue.

7

It wasn't until McNab and the others were on their way back to the township that they spoke.

"Well," McNab said, "we can't do too much here until the autopsy has been done later this afternoon. Officially, we are only here at the invitation of Sergeant Sinclair to observe the body and its place of discovery, on the supposition that this death may not be a natural one. Until it has been proven as such, our squad is not officially in charge of the investigation. In the meantime, let's go back to the Police Station and re-read the statements that have been collected to this time."

He paused, and rubbed his chin.

"On second thoughts, Sarah, I want you to stay here this afternoon at Sunbury. Act as an observer for any further interviews and take notes to keep us up to date. Vincent and I will go to the morgue to observe the autopsy and glean any suspicious results that may show us a possible homicide."

"Okay, boss. I'll sharpen my pencil for the notes," replied Sarah. She looked at Vincent sitting next to her and added, "Good luck with your first autopsy mate!"

"Thanks, Sergeant," replied Vincent, as he pulled up in front of the Police Station. His expression was blank.

"Back so soon?" asked Constable Julie Wiseman as they entered. "The urn over there is hot. Cup of coffee or tea anyone? It's self-service here. Use the polystyrene cups. Milk is in the 'fridge. More importantly, would anyone like me to get a sandwich or something from across the road? You must be getting hungry. It's nearly twelve."

Andy smiled. He then realised that he was rather hungry as it had been a long time since breakfast.

The three detectives gratefully gave their orders and money to Julie. With the list tucked in her top pocket, Julie disappeared.

8

Both detectives were silent during the forty-minute drive south to the city Morgue. Andy guessed that Ng was thinking about the experience ahead. Ng had told him that he had joined the police force mainly as a career in uniform, with ranks to achieve and the respect that went with each succeeding rank. Andy knew that like himself, as a new Australian, there were opportunities to build a new life. On the other hand, Andy McNab realised Ng's challenges with racial differences and acceptance in his new society. He had empathy with Vincent. He knew only too well what it was like to be an immigrant, trying to prove yourself in an adopted country. When he had joined the Australian Police force from the British police, through a recruitment scheme between the United Kingdom and Australia, he had high hopes.

After all, he was going to the land of opportunity. He thought of getting a quick promotion. But that wasn't the case. There had been an undercurrent of jealousy from the Australian members of the force at the time. *Aye,*

*Vincent, I know what it's like. You'll make it, lad.
Perseverance will get you through your problem! And guts--
and you've plenty of that. It took me twenty years to become
a Detective Inspector, but I made it!*

They arrived at the morgue, where McNab
spoke in a quiet, parent-like voice.

"Before we go in, lad, I'll offer a quick word of
advice. I know it's your first time. If you feel sick or
think that you're going to faint, don't panic! Just let
us know and we'll take you outside for some fresh
air. Are you ready?"

Vincent took a deep breath, straightened up his
shoulders, and replied, "Yes, sir."

Once inside, a rather portly gentleman with
glasses perched halfway down his nose, peered at
them. "Hello, Mac," he boomed. "When are you
going to try for the Archibald prize again? I reckon
you'll win next time. Sir John Grey arrived half an
hour ago. He's waiting for you in room two."

"Thanks, Dave. I've nearly finished a portrait
that I might enter this year. I'm having a bit of
trouble getting the finishing touches right, though.
When it's finished, I'll get you to give me your
expert opinion. By the way, Dave, this is Detective
Constable Vincent Ng, the squad's new recruit."

"G'day, Vincent. Don't worry. I'll be standing
next to you. Just let me know if you want to go
outside, eh?" Dave winked at Andy, then looked at
Vincent. "Nothing to be ashamed of," he said, as

they walked down the corridor. "At least seventy-five per cent of the new viewers end up on their backs. Did you know that your boss and I are fellow painters? We did some fine arts subjects together at University. Those body drawing classes were the best, weren't they, mate?"

Room two was similar to an operating theatre. The difference was that the body on the table was not alive. Dave ushered them to an adjoining room where they put on overgarments, and plastic aprons and gloves, ready to be observers.

Half an hour later, Vincent was still on his feet. The skilled hands of Sir John Grey were probing and searching the body. His assistant was kept busy taking various organs to the scales to be weighed, measured, then put into labelled containers for further analysis. Grey's deep voice echoed around the cool room.

"That's strange! There's no water in the lungs. Take a look. It wasn't a heart attack and there are no visible signs of strangulation. No bruising on the neck. Yet, something stopped his heart."

McNab peered to look closer. The individual body organs looked just like photos in medical books. It was as if Sir Peter as a person no longer existed, only these lifeless organs.

Sir John looked up at McNab. "The blood alcohol level shows point zero five, which meant that he shouldn't have driven a car, but was still not enough to make him black out. It may be some kind of poison, but we'll have to wait for the results of toxin tests of the blood and stomach contents."

"Maybe, he had imbibed enough of his beloved whisky to make him relaxed enough in the spa to allow someone to suffocate him? Or perhaps, someone he least suspected drugged him?"

"Possibly, but there are no marks around the face or neck or bruising on the nose to suggest that someone tried to stop him from breathing. Until we get the full analysis of his blood tests, we won't be able to discount possible foul play with the use of drugs, sedatives, or even poison. I must agree, Inspector, with his local doctor that it does look like a suspicious death." Sir John sighed and added, "At this stage, though, I can only confirm his death by causes unknown."

"Thanks, Sir John. We'll wait for the tests. In the meantime, I'll check and see if the local police have found anything in the spa. I asked them to empty it and send a sample to you for analysis."

"Good. I'll test the water myself. I'll let you know as soon as I get the results, McNab."

It was nearly five o'clock by the time they reached the city office. For a long while, the only sounds were the clicking of computer keys and the buzz of the printers as reports were finished. The phone on McNab's desk echoed around the room.

"McNab speaking."

"Hi, boss, it's Sarah. Anything interesting found at the autopsy?"

"No, nothing dramatic so far, except that Grey reckons he died suspiciously. We still have to find out how and why he stopped breathing. The blood tests might show up something."

"Apart from the plastic drinking cup at the spa, we found a small vial-like container in the garden near the side gate."

McNab face broke into a grin and he added, "How interesting! Were there any fingerprints on them?"

"No such luck."

"Damn! I guess we will have to let the forensic team check out the remaining contents. Good work, Sarah. Time to check back here. We'll need a good night's sleep. I have a gut feeling that by tomorrow morning, we will officially have a murder case on our hands, lass." With that remark, McNab hung up the phone.

"Did Sarah find something, sir?" asked Ng.

"Yes, lad. Apart from the empty plastic-drinking cup originally found next to the spa, they've found an empty, vial-like container in the garden near the side gate. The container appears to have no fingerprints on it, though. With a bit of luck, forensic should find that the fingerprints on the cup will match Sir Peter's. They may also find something of interest about the remnants of the contents of the cup and the container."

"Do you think someone murdered Sir Peter? One of the family?" asked Ng.

"Too early to guess yet, Vincent. Tomorrow we will start to learn everything and anything possible about Sir Peter Percival. I had an old Super in Edinburgh who once told me that when investigating murder, there were always four words starting with L that were crucial to the task: Love, Lust, Loathing and Lucre. Once we find our how, then we may be able to find out who the killer is. Sir Peter was a powerful man in business and politics. Privately, he was the strong head of his family. Along the way, he's sure to have made enemies. I've found that most victims knew their murderer. Just like fowls in a Walk, an aspiring Cock sooner or later will challenge the current 'Cock of the Walk' and I guarantee that a lot of feathers will fly around this old Cocks walk before we're through."

9

The phone beside Andy's bed rang loudly at six o'clock the next morning, ending his deep sleep.

"McNab--yes, lass, I'm awake now. What? Bingo! Murder, it is."

He was now wide-awake, his nerves tingling with the familiar excitement that accompanied a new investigation.

"Sarah, pick me up at home. That will save me taking my car over to Sunbury. Do you know where to find my place? That's right. It's the second gate on the left after you turn into Roberts Lane off the main road into Gisborne. You won't miss it. The R.S.D. Box at the gate has two white poodles painted on it. The real dogs will greet you at the gate. Just tell them to get in the back and they can have a ride to the house with you. See you in about an hour, then?"

McNab hung up the phone, got out of bed, let the dogs out for their run and then went to his study. He stood impatiently next to the fax machine.

Now all I need is to read the faxed copy of the autopsy

report. Och, why do these things seem to take forever to come through when you need them?

As if in telepathic answer to his thoughts, the fax machine burst into life, slowly sending out, sheet by sheet, the report that Sarah had promised to send when she had spoken to him on the phone.

He snatched up the last sheet and took the whole pile into the kitchen. After letting the dogs back inside, he put the kettle on, and thumped some bread into the toaster, then started to read the report.

Hmmm, death by asphyxia by poisoning. Maculatum, or poison hemlock. A poisonous dose produces complete paralysis, loss of speech. Respiratory function is first depressed, then ceases, causing death from asphyxia.

Andy quickly scanned the rest of the report as he ate. When he finished, he realised that it was only half an hour before Sarah was due to arrive. He had a strange feeling of anxiousness that he hadn't experienced for years, not since Rhonda had died. It was similar to the feeling he had when Rhonda had called him to say she was coming to visit his flat, before they married. Like a schoolboy about to face his first date--he panicked, rushed to the bathroom to shower and dress, and then began to tidy.

God, you're behaving like a fussy old woman, lad!

He shoved dirty dishes into the dishwasher,

cleared the kitchen bench, and then quickly pulled up the eiderdown on his bed. Even the dogs were not missed, receiving a brisk brush that made them all white and fluffy before he let them outside again. It wasn't long before he heard the dogs barking excitedly in the distance. When he heard car tyres crunching shale in the driveway, he turned the electric jug on for the fourth time and put out two coffee mugs. His fingers trembled as he opened the door.

Damn, it's only Sarah. We see each other every day at work.

He stepped outside to help Sarah let the two energetic dogs out of the car.

"Heck, I've just had my second bath this morning!" she exclaimed, then added, "They're beautiful. What are their names?"

"This one is Snow, the male, and the female is named White." Andy paused, looking embarrassed, then continued, "Rhonda named them when they were eight weeks old. They were two balls of white fluff, then. We had planned to move to this property with the dogs to build a future together-- but that didn't happen. Six weeks after the doctor diagnosed cancer, Rhonda died." Tears welled up in his eyes.

"I was brought up on a farm, sir. I had to move to the big smoke when I did my nursing training. Then, finally, after ten years, and promotion to

Sister at the Royal Melbourne Hospital, I made the career change, joining the force five years ago."

"I know. I've got your resume, remember? Do you like going to the country during your time off?"

"Yes, every chance I get. I like to go bush walking and look at the wildlife, especially birds. I'm no expert, though. There must be some lovely walks around here?"

He broke into a grin. "You're welcome to walk around here anytime, lass!"

"I'm sorry. I didn't mean to sound pushy. I mean, that would be nice." She stopped to look at the paintings hung around the walls of the family room, next to the kitchen. Andrew McNab was the signature on them all. "I didn't know you painted."

Andy watched her as she stopped in front of a painting, sitting on an easel at the end of the family room.

"Oh, I love this one. She's beautiful. Who is she?"

Andy paused, his voice strained when he answered. "Rhonda. I've been trying to finish that portrait for the last five years. I was a finalist in the Archibald Portraiture Prize, with her mother's portrait, seven years ago. Rhonda talked me into it. I've not entered anything since."

"It's very good. Where's the portrait of her mother?"

"The one hanging next to the window over

there," he replied, pointing to the back wall.

Sarah stared in silence at the painting, and Andy knew what she was thinking. He offered an explanation before she asked.

"Her mother's an aborigine. She was beautiful, too. Rhonda's father was a white man," said Andy.

She turned around to face McNab. "No wonder Rhonda was beautiful."

"Aye. Rhonda didn't know who her father was. Her mother would only tell her that he was a city slicker who had worked on a farm nearby where she lived. I believe he was a fiery redhead. I'll never know now, as Rhonda's mother died last year."

"Rhonda's portrait looks fine to me. But you said it's not finished. What still needs to be done?"

"The eyes are not right. I can't get the eyes right, lass." He sighed.

She took a quiet breath and said, "That coffee smells good, sir."

"Hmm, sorry, lass, I forgot to offer some. Here you go."

"Thanks."

They quietly sipped their coffee, each trying not to look directly at the other.

The phone rang, breaking the spell that seemed to have been cast in the room. McNab went into the kitchen, then a minute later, he returned and smiled at Sarah.

"That was Sergeant Sinclair. We're expected at

Woodburne. He's lined up our first interviewee--Joan Wilson, the housekeeper. Joe Wilson, the manager and Sir Peter's children, Jason and Dianne, can be interviewed at the police station. By the way, did you know that Mrs. Wilson is Joe's mother? Time to start sorting out pieces of this murder puzzle, eh?"

Andy was now in work mode. The previous spell of intimacy was gone. Within five minutes, the police car was turning onto the highway, heading towards Sunbury and the mansion of Woodburne.

10

It was nearly 8 o'clock by the time Andy and Sarah arrived at the front gates of Woodburne. Sergeant Sinclair was waiting for them, standing beside his car with Senior Constable Collotti.

"G'day, Andy, Sergeant."

"'Morning, Dennis, Frank," replied McNab. "You certainly picked an interesting time to start work at Sunbury, Frank."

"Yes, sir. I'm looking forward to learning how the homicide squad works," replied Collotti.

McNab nodded. "Let's get going. Looks like it's going to be a long day of interviews ahead of us."

The two cars slowly made their way up the winding driveway that led to the imposing mansion of Woodburne. They parked at the front entrance and walked up the few steps onto the front veranda. It was Sergeant Sinclair who pressed the bell. A few minutes later, a middle-aged woman opened the door. She was an attractive brunette with grey tips showing through her scalp, where the hair under the dye had grown. Her brown eyes were red and her face was flushed from crying. She ushered them inside.

"Please come in, Sergeant. The place is a bit disorganised I'm afraid."

Sergeant Sinclair started introductions but Joan interrupted him.

"Hello again, Inspector," she said, looking at Andy. "I've got the kettle on. Would anyone like a cup of tea or coffee?"

"Yes," Sarah replied. "We would love something, thanks very much. I'm Detective Sergeant Sarah Sedgewick. I'll give you a hand."

Sarah and Joan left the room, and a short time later, Sarah returned, tray in hand. Joan followed, holding a large plate of hot scones, with what looked like homemade jam and cream. They smelled delicious.

"There you are," Joan said. "I thought you might like something to eat. I always feel that at times like this, life must go on for the living. Possibly a strange reaction by me in your eyes, Inspector, but cooking the scones has kept my mind busy, anyway. Please, help yourselves." She quietly sat down opposite McNab and sipped at her cup of black tea.

Andy looked at her. "Mrs. Wilson, I know that you're upset, but if you feel up to it, we need to ask a few questions."

"Certainly, Inspector. Ask away. I think I need to get everything inside me out into the open anyway. I don't know how I will be able to help you, though. I had no idea that anyone would want to hurt Sir Peter, let alone murder him. I feel sorry for poor Lady Laura. It has all been too much for her. She's never been a strong person. She's still sedated you know."

"Mrs. Wilson, tell me what you've seen and heard since yesterday, when you were told by Joe that he had found Sir Peter's body. I've read the statement that you made to Sergeant Sinclair, but maybe you might have remembered something since. Tell me anything, even if you don't think that it may be important."

Andy McNab was using his usual, quiet, but gentle, charm technique that he used so often with bereaved women. It worked every time. The witness often seemed to remember or say something that often proved to be very important.

"I had only just arrived yesterday morning. I was putting on the kettle for Lady Laura's morning cup of tea, when I heard Joe's car coming up the driveway after his usual morning drive around the vineyard. Joe is very methodical. After he checks the vines, he always comes up to the house to see Sir Peter, to co-ordinate any work that needs to be done. He usually comes in through the back door first, gives me a quick hug, and says hello. He doesn't live at home, you see. He lives in the manager's cottage that's down the hill, near the creek."

Joan paused and gulped a large mouthful of tea, then continued.

"Yesterday, he came in as usual, but he looked terrible. He was dry retching. He rushed past me, grabbed the phone and dialled emergency. You know, I don't think I will ever forget what he said to me after he had told the police to come. He said, 'Christ, mum, he's dead in the spa. He looks like a boiled pig!' I didn't realise who he was talking about at first." She paused, shaking.

"Yes, please, when you are ready," McNab said, smiling, then added, "These scones are wonderful! I must get your recipe sometime. They're nicer that the ones my mother used to bake."

Joan relaxed a little, took another gulp of her tea and continued.

"Well, the police came within fifteen minutes. I didn't go out the back when they came. I didn't want to see Sir Peter in the spa. I want to remember him from the time when he was alive. I don't like seeing dead people at the best of times. It's not that I haven't in my day, you know. I do a lot of charity work in the local district. I've discovered a few old folk dead in bed during my meals-on-wheels run. Maybe it was different with them, because their time was due and it was always peaceful."

She paused again to compose herself, and

continued as if she had to get everything off her chest in one sitting, like a confession at church.

"The rest of the day, I kept myself busy, cleaning up the kitchen, answering calls at the door and on the phone. Late yesterday, I rang my husband at the Bank and told him that I was going to stay overnight, as Lady Laura was extremely stressed. Jason had told her about Sir Peter's death. I thought he was very good to tell her in such a gentle way. Poor Jason is not a very confident person. Not like his father. Sir Peter was a born leader. He was always so confident. Everyone respected him. I don't know about enemies though. Even everyone at the Farmers Co-op supported him when he called for an inquiry into the discrepancy in the funds. My husband Roger will be able to tell you more about the Co-op's problems, Inspector. He's the local Bank Manager and the Co-op Treasurer--of course, you know that already--sorry I forgot, you already met my husband when you were making inquiries about the corruption reports. Sorry--where was I?"

"You were telling us about deciding to stay the night here, Mrs. Wilson," prompted McNab.

"Oh, yes. Well, Roger told me that it was a good idea. We both knew how unstable Lady Laura was. I hadn't intended to hold her hand all night. I only meant to be available if she needed someone, that's all. Anyway, she didn't want to eat anything all day.

She refused to see Doctor Poulter, who had asked if she needed a sedative or anything for the shock. In fact, she was quite blunt in asking me to refuse his assistance. Her exact words were, 'Tell that nosy Doctor to piss off!' I didn't repeat her exact words to the doctor!" She sighed, and added, "The doctor gave me some sedation pills for her anyway."

McNab leaned forward in his chair. "Did you go out the back door when you arrived yesterday?"

"No! Why should I? I usually don't go out of the back door until Joe is leaving."

McNab kept probing. "So you didn't hear the spa?"

"No! I'm a bit hard of hearing; maybe that's why I didn't hear it."

Andy thought, *hard of hearing, but still able to hear your son's car coming up the drive out the front?*

Joan had turned pale. She slumped back into her chair.

Sergeant Sinclair went over to her. "Are you all right, Joan? Can I pour you another cuppa?"

"Thanks, Dennis. I feel a little dizzy."

Damn! That's as far as we can go today without being accused of taking advantage of a sick witness. Och, I know she's keeping something back.

Andy McNab got up. Sarah followed. It was obvious that Joan Wilson had had quite enough, for this session anyway. McNab smiled briefly at her. "Thanks for telling us what you saw. I'll catch up with you when you've rested. You look as if you need to get away from here and rest at home. Perhaps Dennis can give you a lift. By the way, I meant what I said about your scone recipe. I'll keep nagging you for it."

Andy and Sarah stepped out into the hallway and then into the warm, sunny day outside.

"She didn't really have anything different to tell us that isn't in the statement made to Sergeant Sinclair yesterday, boss," remarked Sarah.

"It's not what she said, lass; it's what she didn't say. I think she's deliberately holding back. She knows a lot about the Percival family. She hasn't worked for them for nearly twenty-four years without knowing about some possible skeletons in their family cupboard. I guess time may help us to probe out more from the devoted Joan."

Sarah looked back and said, "You think they are all 'Birds of a feather' don't you, and they'll stick together!"

"Aye, that's just what I'm afraid of."

With that last remark, McNab opened the car door, swung his long legs in, and waited for Sarah to drive him back to the Sunbury Police Station.

BOOK TWO
Cockshy

11

As McNab unwound his tall frame out of the police car, he noticed that Ng had arrived from head office in Melbourne.

"Let's see what information Vincent has been able to scrounge up for our files," he said, winking at Sarah as they walked into the Sunbury Police Station entrance.

"Well, he went to see Sir Peter Percival's solicitor this morning first thing. Maybe there's something in Sir Peter's will that'll point us in the right direction?"

"I'd be surprised if the will's contents reveal anything dramatic. Then again, nothing would surprise me, especially when murder is involved."

They went inside the police station. Vincent Ng stood up when they entered the main office behind the reception area.

"Ah! Vincent," McNab said, "find out anything interesting, lad?"

"Yes, sir. I've found out that Sir Peter visited his solicitor two weeks ago to change his will. The new will included a new, major beneficiary--Joseph Wilson. Puts a cat among the pigeons, doesn't it?"

McNab smiled at Vincent's enthusiasm and took the document that Ng offered to him, replying quietly, "More correctly, it's put a fox in the hen house!"

They went into an adjacent office set aside for their use during the investigation. McNab read the copy of the Final Will and Testament of Sir Peter Percival with quiet interest for a few minutes, then looked up at Vincent and Sarah with a frown on his face.

"Joe Wilson and Jason Percival are to become equal owners of the Woodburne Winery. Lady Laura is to have life rent of the Estate and, upon her death, Joe and Jason take over the lot. Dianne Gambello, his daughter, and her husband Fredrico are to receive a lump sum payment and a large trust for their future children. Two other interesting features are a lump sum to Joan Wilson and a fund to establish a scholarship through the local farmers Co-op for Viticulture Studies at the Victoria University campus in Sunbury. Any comments?"

"Joe Wilson discovered the body," Sarah said. "He was alone in his cottage all night and has no alibi, which makes him a prime suspect. Then again, if Jason knew about the new will, he would be a perfect suspect, being jealous of Joe's new share of the estate."

"The will's contents won't be officially known until tomorrow, when the family and beneficiaries are to be advised at the solicitors Sunbury office," interrupted Vincent.

McNab looked grimly at his colleagues. "So, we need to find out who knew about this new will and its contents prior to his murder! Maybe someone preferred the old one. This may or may not be--"

Constable Julie Wiseman came into the room, interrupting McNab's comments. She carried a plate of donuts.

"'Morning, everyone. Thought you'd be hungry," she clucked, setting the plate down.

"Err, 'morning, Julie. Thanks," replied McNab.

Julie smiled and bustled out again, oblivious to the fact that she had stopped McNab's train of thought. Vincent immediately grabbed a doughnut and started to devour it, then looked at his two companions who were grinning at him.

"Something wrong? Aren't you two hungry?"

"Joan Wilson supplied us with homemade scones," McNab explained. "If this investigation takes more than a week of our time up here, we'll be waddling back to Melbourne like fat Christmas Turkeys."

"Eat my share, Vincent, so Julie won't be offended," groaned Sarah.

Vincent nodded and took another mouthful.

McNab sighed. "After our earlier conversation, Sarah, I'm beginning to wonder if Joan Wilson is trying to protect Joe in some way. Also, why is she, an 'outsider' getting such a large, lump sum in the will?"

"For service rendered as the housekeeper?" suggested Vincent.

"Maybe she offered special extra services, apart from those of housekeeper," offered Sarah.

"Now that would be something, lass, especially right under the nose of Lady Laura!" snorted McNab.

There was a knock at the door. Julie Wiseman came in, looked at McNab and formally announced, "Joe Wilson's here. He's waiting for you in the interview room sir,"

"Thanks constable," he replied. Turning to Sarah and Vincent he added, "Right, let's go a talk to Joseph Wilson."

12

Joe Wilson stood up when they entered the interview room. His ruffled brown hair and deep blue eyes that peered at them from below sun bleached eyebrows, accentuated the tanned, handsome face.

"Joe, I'm Detective Inspector Andy McNab, this is Detective Sergeant Sarah Sedgewick and Detective Constable Vincent Ng. Please sit. Although you've already spoken to the local police and signed a statement, we need to ask you a few more questions to clarify a few things." McNab thought, *Well lad, I can't say you look exactly comfortable. That's good--I need you to be a little nervous.*

McNab sat down opposite Joe at the table, with Sarah next to him, she with notepad in hand. Vincent pressed the tape recorder's start button, recited the names of those present, and then advised Joe of his legal rights.

"You have the right to have a solicitor present, Joe. Do you want to go ahead without one present?" asked McNab.

"No, I'm fine." Joe's voice echoed around the room as he continued, barely pausing for breath. "I dreamt about it--it was awful--just like I found him--same staring eyes--the steam. I couldn't breathe." The words tumbled out, and although it was cool in the room, he was beginning to sweat.

McNab looked directly at Joe and said calmly, "Dream? You didn't mention anything about a dream in your statement, Joe. Tell me about it."

"The dream woke me up early yesterday morning. It was so real. All I can remember was a clammy steam, then hot, bubbling water. A large pink blob with staring eyes bounced up at me through the steam." Joe stopped, and wiped the back of his right hand across his brow. His gaze darted around the room.

"So this dream happened before you found Sir Peter's body? Did you recognize Sir Peter in the dream, Joe?" asked McNab.

"No, Inspector! I didn't even know that it was a body--or a spa--in the dream, I mean. It was only when I saw Sir Peter's body floating in the spa that the dream became real. I haven't been able to sleep properly since."

"Perhaps you should ask your Doctor to organise something to help you, Joe. Premonitions are a bit out my league," replied McNab. *Now's the time to ask him about the will,* he thought. "Joe, are you aware of the contents of Sir Peter's latest will?"

"Latest will? You mean there's been more than one? No, I know nothing about Sir Peter's private matters, Inspector. Why should I? Jason's told me that their solicitor wants me to go to their office tomorrow morning. Perhaps they need me there to clarify the business queries. Jason is the sales person. He relied on me to run the business. So did Sir Peter. They trusted me. That suited me, too. It's better than having non-experts telling you what to do.

Andy noted that Joe sounded more confident and in better control of his feelings. "Sir Peter and Jason were not experts in their own wine business?" he asked.

"You're twisting my words, Inspector. What I meant was that my job is to run the business as a trained vintner. Sir Peter and Jason are not vintners. It's as simple as that." Joe scowled across the table as he said the last sentence.

So, McNab thought, *you think that you're superior in knowledge to your employers', lad.* "You must have been close to Sir Peter to have such a dream. Were you and Jason both close?"

"I guess we were. He treated me more like another son than his manager at times. Jason, his son, is a good friend and together we basically run the Vineyard. As I've already said, Jason does the sales, while I'm the vintner. Sir Peter is--was the figurehead." Joe stopped talking, and rested his head on his hands, propped on the table.

"You're young to be in charge of such a famous

vineyard. You must have been highly recommended," stated McNab. He waited for the reaction. It was a confident reply.

"Yes, I'm one of the youngest managers in the state. I was the top student at the Melbourne Technical College. I graduated in Viticulture and management two years ago. Sir Peter offered me the position straight after I finished college. I guess my appointment was a surprise to some of the locals. They probably thought that Jason should have been the official manager, but the truth is that Jason didn't want the job. He's happier letting me do the paperwork, although he likes me to help him with the sales side, too. He isn't as confident as I am, I guess. We've been mates all through school and college. Jason is two years younger than I am. He decided to do the marketing course, at the same time I was at Agricultural College."

"Joe, you said in your statement that you were alone the night before and that you have no one to support your alibi."

"Only Sooty my cat, and he can't speak for me. I live alone, Inspector. It's normal for me to be alone at night." Joe looked down at his hands, avoiding Andy's penetrating eyes.

"Did you notice anything strange or different when you first entered the back yard yesterday?"

"Strange? No, Inspector, I don't think so I only remember thinking to myself that it wasn't like the boss to leave the spa on. I mean on overnight. He always had an evening swim, summer, or winter, followed by a spa. I heard the spa bubbling in the morning, and that wasn't normal. So I went straight to the spa room to check it--that's when I found the boss. It's weird, but I instantly thought that it was murder. I can't explain why. It was murder wasn't it?"

Andy was silent for a moment. *Time to get back in control of this interview, Andy. Change tactics. Ask some personal questions to put him back on the defensive.* "You live alone. Do you have a girlfriend?"

"What? What's this to do with Sir Peter's death?"

"Please answer the question."

"Hey, Inspector, I'm not gay, and I certainly don't live like a monk! I don't have a serious girlfriend at the moment, but I do have a wide circle of friends, along with Jason Percival. Most of our group of friends went to school with us. In a small country-style town like Sunbury, we all tend to group together. Some have drifted off to the big smoke to earn a living, but most seem to return to visit their grass roots. It's a close community."

McNab smiled at Joe. "Have you had any serious relationship that might have caused some jealousy amongst the locals? Don't misunderstand this last question, but I need to know if anyone might want to cause harm to anyone at

Woodburne."

"You mean, if Sir Peter was murdered, he may not have been the intended victim? God, I hadn't thought of that. Hell, I think I'd better tell you that I was in love a couple of years ago, with Dianne Percival. We were childhood sweethearts sort of-- you know--close school buddies. She's only four months younger than I am. Dianne, Jason and I went everywhere together. When my parents and Dianne's parents found out that it was getting serious, they split us up."

"Oh, why?"

"They said we were too young. I went to College. Dianne spat the dummy and left her family circle the next day and lived in a local flat with a girlfriend. Six months later, she was engaged to Fredrico Gambello. Fred's father owns a vineyard. They produce excellent wine. Fred and Dianne married last year, in a quiet garden setting at Woodburne. I was invited."

"Did you go?"

"Of course I went. I wasn't jealous. They seem quite happy together, but keep away from Sir Peter and Lady Laura. Dianne seems to be glad of her independence. The Gambello's are a wealthy family, so she's kept in the style that she was brought up in."

Andy noted the slight bitterness in the last remark. "Did Sir Peter have any enemies that you know of?"

Joe hesitated. "Um, no, not that I know about. Being a politician, I guess there could be people who didn't like his politics."

Aye, that's a loyal lad. Keep yourself politically on the same side as your employers' Damn it, you're a cocky bastard! "We'll stop these questions for now, Joe. We reserve the right to call you in again."

Joe got up, smiled briefly, and then without another word, left the room.

Sarah stood up, stretching her arms. "I wonder if Joe was really angry enough to want to kill Sir Peter for breaking up his romance with Dianne?"

"Only time will tell. We have no hard evidence against him--for now anyway. However, he's not in the clear. He's certainly loyal to the Percival family. I'm curious to know why the two families were so keen to stop that relationship though. Perhaps Jason or Dianne can add a few extra pieces to our jigsaw puzzle. I think we are going to find a few *cockshy* people around this close community. They'll try to protect each other. We'll have to find a weak link somewhere."

There was a knock on the door. and Julie entered with a blonde woman Andy noted that she looked exactly as he imagined Lady Laura would have been about twenty five years earlier. It was Dianne Gambello, Sir Peter's daughter.

13

After the formal introductions, McNab started the questioning. "Dianne, I'm sorry about your father's death. I know it's a bad time for you at the moment, but we need to ask you some questions to help us get a clearer picture."

Dianne fluttered her eyelids revealing a pair of green eyes. "You don't have to worry about my feelings, Inspector."

"Oh, why not?

"I haven't been close to my parents for over two years." She slouched back in her chair, arms folded, her lower lip pouting

Och, you may look like your mother lass, but I bet you have your father's stubbornness. "So, you're not sad that your father's dead?"

"No, I'm glad he's dead. I hated him!" She spat out the words like a snarling cat ready for a fight.

McNab's voice remained calm. "Why did you hate your father?"

"He never had any time for me. I was only a girl. He always favoured Jason. Even Joe got more attention from my father than I did." She peered up at McNab, her eyes brimming with tears. "He didn't love me, you see. I hate him--hate him. I'm glad he's dead."

"Did you hate him enough to want to kill him?"

"What? Get real, Inspector. I said I hated the old man. He drowned in his bloody spa. It's as simple as that. But, I didn't hate him enough to want to kill. He drowned, didn't he?" She paused, looking from one to the other. "Oh God, are you asking me these questions because he was murdered? Oh no, Daddy was murdered?" She burst into hysterical crying.

Vincent's voice dictated into the tape, "This interview is suspended at 10.15am for a coffee break."

Sarah went out and brought back a cup of coffee. She handed it to the now sniffing Dianne. "Here's a packet of sugar and a stirrer, if you need it."

"Thanks, I'm sorry. I was so nervous and angry about having to come here."

McNab sat down opposite Dianne. He smiled briefly at her, but not enough for her to take advantage over him. "Dianne, we need to ask some more questions. Do you want to continue?"

"Yes. I'm fine now." She fluttered her eyelids at McNab and smiled.

I bet you have a fiery temper lass. The tape restarted and he spoke with a calm voice. "Dianne, where were you yesterday?"

"With Ma."

"Ma?"

"Ma Gambello, my mother-in-law."

"Where were you and what were you doing."

"You want an alibi, don't you? Well I've got one, so there." Dianne scowled.

McNab felt like shouting at her, or shaking her. *You're certainly spoilt, lass.* He took a deep breath, then continued calmly "Dianne, I know it's not pleasant being asked personal questions, but it's our job to check everyone's movements, especially those associated with your father during the last twenty-four hours."

The truculent beauty emitted a deep, dramatic sigh. She unfolded her arms and stuffed her hands into the pockets of her jeans. The pouting lip started to quiver. "Ma and I, I mean Mrs Gambello and I, were busy preparing the wine-tasting bar for the day. That's when Jason rang from Woodburne and told us about Daddy. The local police came about ten minutes later. I spent the morning being questioned by them."

"Where was your husband?"

"Fredrico was back at home in bed. He had a gastric upset. He'd been chucking up all night, which kept me awake for hours. He said he was too sick to work yesterday. Anyway I went to the farm to work, even though I only got a few winks myself. Ma needs me to help her."

"You like your mother-in-law?"

"Of course, I do."

The face was now showing signs of anger. She stopped talking for a moment. She seemed to be trying to control her temper. There was another deep sigh. She took her hands out of her jeans pockets and crossed them on the table in front of her.

"I'm sorry, Inspector. Fred is always ticking me off about my short fuse. I love my mother-in-law. She's more of a mother to me than my real mother. We have fun together. She's got a wicked sense of humour."

"What did you do after the police left?"

"Ma took me home to Fred. He was up watching tennis on TV. I spent the rest of the day with him."

McNab leant back, watching the sultry blond, thinking how much like her mother she was. The main difference was that Dianne had some life and fire in her. When he dined at Woodburne, Lady Laura, in comparison, was beautiful, but vacant and without any animation. He wondered if Lady Laura had once had this same zeal shown by her daughter.

"Do you know of anyone who might have had a grudge against your father or about any recent arguments he might have had with anyone?"

"Some of his ex employees could be put on a list. My father wasn't always the nice guy everyone saw. How do you think he got to the top of the ladder in the business world? My nickname for him was 'hatchet man'. He often sacked people who got in his way or didn't agree with his ideas. There were others in the farmers Co-op who didn't like him either." She stopped again and took another deep breath. "I know I sound bitter, but all the time I lived at home, he was so ambitious. He was always hungry for success and money. And power, I guess. It's funny, you know, but it's only now that I've realised that all my father really wanted was power over everything he owned or organised."

McNab looked at Dianne closely. "So you resented your father?"

"No, but I used to, before I married. I was so pissed off when he split up Joe and me. Joe's still a good mate. Fred likes him, too. It's just that my father is...I mean, was...always sticking his nose into other people's lives. Mummy is probably the lucky one. She doesn't really understand that Daddy is dead. She hasn't slept in the same room with him for twenty-five years--since her breakdown." She suddenly looked embarrassed.

Ah, a family secret revealed--good!

"I probably shouldn't have told you that. It's really none of your business." She pouted again. "You don't think much of me, do you?"

"What makes you think that, Dianne?"

"The look in your eyes, Inspector!"

"Have you visited or seen your parents recently?"

"Two days ago Fred and I went to see Mummy. She wasn't very well. She had a stomach upset. I think that's who gave it to Fred. Mummy, as you know, is not a--a well person. She had a nervous breakdown after Jason was born. I don't remember this, as I was only two at the time. She's never really recovered. Just spends her days pottering in her glasshouse, or in her room, listening to music, pumping herself with dope and sleeping. I know this sounds bad, but she seems happy enough. After all, she's still my mother. But I can't really say that I feel close to her. I feel closer to Joan Rogers. She more or less brought Jason and me up, together with Joe."

"Were you angry when your parents stopped your relationship with Joe?" asked Sarah.

"Angry enough to want to kill my father? Don't be stupid. He was my father, after all. No, I didn't want my father killed." She looked at her watch and frowned. "Anything else you want to know? I need to get back to help Ma at the farm."

"Did you kill your father?"

"No!"

She glowered at McNab, who stood up and said, "That's all for now, Dianne. However we may need to see you again sometime."

The interview was over. Dianne got up, flicked her long hair back out of her face, and then stalked out of the room, slamming the door behind her.

Sarah looked a McNab and whistled softly, saying, "Spoilt bitch."

"Spoilt or not, she has a fiery temper," commented McNab.

"Interesting comments she made about her father's attitudes to his employees and opponents, sir," remarked Vincent.

"Aye, lad. It now looks like there might be a long line of people who wanted him out of the way.

Another knock on the door, and this time Julie came in with cups of coffee and a plate of chocolate biscuits. McNab grinned. *I'll put on weight with all these snacks. Still, her heart's in the right place.*

As Julie put the plate on the table, she said, "I thought you three might want a little sustenance between interviews. Jason Percival is ready when you are, sir. Just let me know and I'll show him in."

"Thanks, constable. We'll be about five minutes. I'll let you know when we're ready."

Julie left the room. McNab sipped his coffee gratefully, then grinning said, "Biscuit anyone?"

14

"How old are you, Jason?" asked McNab.

"You know my age. It's on the top of my statement that you've got in front of you." Jason pushed his hands into his pockets, reflecting the same petulant, defensive stance of his sister Dianne.

Andy McNab was beginning to realise that, in Jason's eyes, he was only a civil servant. As such he was a lower human being on the 'Percival Social Scale'. He felt a rising resentment welling up inside and thought, *Young upstart! I could argue the toss with you, lad. I'm better educated. I have a University Bachelor of Arts in Sociology and Fine Arts. I'm a respected artist. I went to Glenalmond, one of the top boarding schools in Scotland. Who the hell do you think you are?*

McNab quietly eyeballed Jason. He took a deep breath to control his temper and clenched his teeth. Jason's pale blue eyes stared back defiantly at McNab for a few moments, then diverted away and looked down at the table. Andy noted that Jason's golden-red hair was immaculately groomed and shining with health, but the freckled face was now slightly pale as he said quietly, "I'm twenty-three, Inspector. Dianne is twenty months older."

"We need to know your movements from yesterday evening until the time your father was found in the spa."

"I had a drink with dad about seven. We had an argument. After we had both calmed down, I left, around seven thirty and went to the local Railway Pub. You probably already know about that anyway. The local busy bodies were all eyes when I got drunk later. I stayed at the pub and had something to eat, then drank until closing time. Mike and Mavis poured me into a local cab and sent me home. I don't remember much after that. I guess I went to bed when I got home. I went for a ride at seven in the morning. I waved at Joe in the paddock. Joan met me after my ride. She was in a terrible state. She told me Dad was dead and that Joe had called the police."

"What was the argument about, Jason?" asked McNab.

"It wasn't really an argument."

"Oh? What would you call it then?"

"It was more like a heated discussion. I was angry with dad. Angry is probably putting it mildly--I was pissed off. He had asked me to his study for a drink and chat. This so-called chat was to tell me that he had changed his will."

"He told you about the new will's contents?"

"Yes."

"What did he tell you?"

Jason sighed, and leaned forward in his chair. "He told me that Joe Wilson was going to be a beneficiary in the will."

"Did that surprise you?"

"Of course it did! I like Joe. He's my best friend, as well as being the manager of the vineyard. But why was Dad handing him half share of the estate?"

"Did he explain why, Jason?"

"No, he didn't. That pissed me off even more than before. Yeah, on second thought, I guess it was an argument. I asked him why Joe was now included in the half share instead of Dianne, like the first will. He just smiled and smugly said that all in good time, when the will came into action, we would all find out. Can you imagine how I felt? I was angrier for Dianne than myself. After all, I was only getting half share in the original will. Mum still had the same deal of an income as long as she lived at the farm and didn't remarry. The main difference was that Dianne, in the new will, loses her half share and instead gets a huge lump sum and a trust fund, set up for future children. The bastard had never forgiven Dianne for marrying beneath her social standing, so to speak. Dad is--um--was a domineering pig--and a racist. He found it hard to swallow that his beautiful daughter was marrying an

Italian's son. Christ, Fred was born in Sunbury. I went to school with him. He's a great bloke who's done wonders for Dianne. So has Mrs. Gambello. She's lovely. A wicked sense of humour, but..." Jason stopped talking, as if he was trying to control his temper.

"Does Dianne know all this?"

"No, not that I'm aware of. He planned to tell her sometime today. I guess she'll find out everything, like I will, at the solicitors when the full will is finally read. Shit, it's such a bloody mess!"

Aye, it is a mess all right. But why choose Joe above Dianne?

Joe cleared his throat and said, "I wouldn't put it past the old bugger to have chosen Joe instead of Dianne, because he's a male. Dad was such a chauvinistic, patriarchal old coot. He never let mum have anything to do with the vineyard. He used to say, 'It's not women's work!' Hell, it's just like him to organise us all from his grave."

"Did you want to kill your father?"

"What?"

"Let me ask you more bluntly, Jason. Did you kill your father?"

"He was murdered? He didn't drown? Shit, what a mess. No, I didn't kill him. I may have thought about it, but I didn't kill him. You won't be able to prove anything anyway. I have an alibi."

"It's not an airtight alibi, Jason. We only have

your word that you left your father alive before going to the pub. It's also only your word that you went straight to bed when you arrived home." McNab looked at Ng and asked, "Vincent, could you check with Sergeant Sinclair and see if they have located the taxi driver who took Jason home?"

"Yes, sir." Vincent stood up. "For the tape, Detective Constable Ng is leaving the room." With those words, Ng left.

McNab then looked at Jason Percival and said, "I'll ask you once more, Jason. Did you kill you father?"

"No! No! No!" shouted Jason, thumping his fists down on the table. "Even if I had, I wouldn't admit it to you."

"I'm terminating this interview now, Jason. We reserve the right to talk to you again," said McNab.

"Thanks for nothing," snarled Jason as he stomped out of the room.

"And we thought Dianne had a fiery temper. Hah, Jason makes her look like a tame pussycat," remarked Sarah.

"Hmm? Sorry, Sarah. What did you say?"

"Nothing important. Where do we go now? We have already talked with three young people who have every motive and desire to want Sir Peter dead. None of them have reliable alibis. We also have the added puzzle of Jason being added to the new Will, so far without any explanation."

"Aye, lass. All we can do at the moment is collect these pieces of the final jigsaw and hope that eventually they will fall into place."

"Maybe Lady Laura can give us a reason for Joe's inclusion in the Will. I wonder if she's available to be questioned yet."

"Let's find out, shall we?" he replied.

McNab and Sedgewick left the interview room and headed towards Sinclair's office down the hall.

15

Sergeant Dennis Sinclair's tummy bounced as he stood up at his desk when they entered. "I've been reading a faxed copy of the autopsy report. I guess you have a copy already?"

"Yes thanks, Dennis, I was faxed one early this morning at home," replied McNab.

"Poison hemlock, eh--unusual, isn't it?" asked Sinclair.

"I gather it was not an uncommon method in the dark ages, Dennis. The plastic vial that Sarah found had the same remnants of poison hemlock that were found in Sir Peter's plastic tumbler," replied McNab.

"Would the fact that a medical style vial was used to carry to poison mean that the murderer is medically trained, or a pharmacist?" asked Sarah.

"That's a possibility, Sarah. However it may also mean that the murderer obtained the hemlock from someone with such training," replied McNab.

"Has anyone thought that a herbalist or a naturopath prepared the hemlock? The Vietnamese, Chinese and other Asian herbalists are experts in preparing weird, ancient, and wonderful potions," remarked Ng.

"Good one, Vincent. You can check any herbalists and Naturopaths operating around here," responded McNab.

Ng blushed. "Yes, boss!"

McNab smiled inwardly. It was the first time that Vincent had called him by the more familiar title of 'boss'. *Good, lad, you're getting the hang of being one of my team.*

"Sir John says its asphyxia by poisoning," said McNab, then continued before anyone could make a comment. "I'll read the explanation from the report so we all have it fresh in our minds before continuing our investigation.

"Conium Maculatum or common name is Poison Hemlock, a member of the Umbelliferai, the same family of plants as parsley, fennel, parsnip, and carrot. The fresh leaves and fruit contain a volatile, oily alkaloid, so poisonous that a few drops prove fatal to a small animal. Inhalation is said to relieve cough in bronchitis, whooping cough, and asthma. It has to be administered with care as narcotic poisoning may result from internal use, producing paralysis. A poisonous dose produces complete paralysis, loss of speech. Respiratory function is first depressed then ceases, causing death from asphyxia." McNab looked up briefly, then continued. "Sir John then says, 'I have taken into account, the spa's water temperature, Sir Peter's body temperature, the start of rigor mortis and finally the amount of the alkaloid poison in the blood stream. The possible ingestion of the poison can be narrowed down to sometime in the early evening of Sir Peter's death. Death possibly occurred between 7pm and 10pm. Death was Asphyxia, by poison. That's why there was no water in the lungs. He was dead before he submerged under the water.'" Andy was suddenly aware that everyone was watching him, dwelling on everything that he had said.

Senior constable Frank Collotti entered the room, and looked at Dennis Sinclair. "Sorry to interrupt, Sergeant, but you wanted me to remind you when it's time to go to Woodburne with Inspector McNab to listen to the interview with Lady Laura. She's the only member of the Percival family who has not given a statement, let alone been interviewed."

"That's right," replied Sinclair who appeared to be a little embarrassed. He looked a McNab and said, "My fault in not asking you first, Andy, but I knew you wouldn't mind. Frank has been coordinating all the statements up until your arrival on the scene, as you know."

"No need to apologise, Dennis. Frank, you are welcome to sit in on the interview with Lady Laura. I have a lot of unanswered questions that I'd like to ask her. Let's hope she's up to it," said McNab.

Julie Wiseman came in with a large plate of sandwiches. "Thought you would all like a snack before you go to Woodburne."

McNab looked at his watch. It was nearly midday. It seemed hard to believe that the morning had already gone. In spite of his promise to himself to stop eating all the 'Wiseman Snacks', he realised that he was hungry. Everyone else also seemed to be hungry and started to devour the offerings on the plate.

Fifteen minutes later, McNab, Ng, Sedgewick, and Collotti left the Sunbury Police Station and headed towards the mansion on the hill.

16

Collotti was a good driver. Ng sat in the front beside him while McNab and Sedgewick sat in the back. Ten minutes later, they arrived at the front gates, then drove up the steep, winding driveway to the front of the mansion. Joan Wilson was waiting for them on the front veranda. She was wiping her hands on her apron.

"Saw the car coming up the drive. Hello, Inspector." She beamed at McNab.

He couldn't help but like this woman, but he mentally cautioned himself. *Was your dizzy spell an act this morning? Be careful, Andy. She is still a suspect. Keep your distance, lad, but keep her happy. She must know some family secrets.* He smiled politely back. "Hello, Joan. I'm surprised you're still here. You look a lot better than earlier. Hope you have a copy of that scone recipe."

"Not written out, Inspector. It's all in my head. I'll write it out for you tonight. Come in. I'll let Lady Laura know that you're here. Let's hope she's in a better mood than earlier today."

She took them inside to the same spacious

lounge room that they had been in during Joan's early morning interview, then left them and disappeared up the huge, dark, Gothic-style staircase.

McNab wondered if Lady Laura was still the beautiful woman that he had remembered, sitting opposite him just over two weeks previously when he had dined at Woodburne. She had the same exotic green eyes that her daughter Dianne had inherited. Yes, young Dianne was definitely her child. *Strange how my original opinion of Sir Peter is beginning to change. The man that I basically liked and admired on the surface, is now being shown as a man not liked or respected by his family. I wonder if Lady Laura will now reveal some more information. I need her opinion to help to confirm these feelings.*

An unearthly scream from upstairs invaded his pondering. McNab, Ng, Collotti, and Sedgewick all rushed up the staircase together, bumping each other like a rugby scrum scrambling for a ball. McNab managed to squeeze past Collotti to be the first to enter the room at the end of the passageway, where the screams were coming from.

Joan Wilson was standing beside a king-sized bed where Lady Laura lay, curled up in a foetal position. An envelope was clutched in her right hand. There was an empty glass, half-empty whisky bottle and an empty vial on the bedside table.

Joan looked at the group coming into the

bedroom and swaying on her feet croaked, "She's dead!" She then staggered towards McNab and collapsed in a deep faint into his waiting arms.

17

Sarah was downstairs. She sat next to Joan who sipped some sweet tea but had managed to tell her, between sobs and sniffs, that Lady Laura had eaten some toast around nine, then asked her to go and leave her alone to prepare for the afternoon interview.

Doctor Poulter was on his way, so for McNab, who had remained upstairs, it was now simply a matter of waiting for Lady Laura to be officially declared dead.

Ng looked a McNab and asked, "Is Lady Laura's death suspicious?"

"According to the letter she was holding, it looks like suicide. The writing has to be verified by the experts, of course. It's a sad, last testament for such a person to leave as their epitaph. I'll read out what she wrote.

"*'To whom it may concern,*

I killed my husband. It's my entire fault. I put something in his whisky that he drank. He didn't know. I wanted to help him relax. He had been tense all week, and had complained that he hadn't been sleeping properly. He was anxious about his new will. He wouldn't tell me what was in the new will. He took the whisky and told me to leave him alone. He drowned in the spa because of me. I want my family to know that it was an accident. All I have given my husband for twenty years is sadness. He wouldn't let me near him. He wanted me to stay in the house or in my room. That made me more depressed and helpless.

My specialist hasn't been able to help me. I'm tired of the constant pills and consultations. I'm no use to anyone any more. I can't live with the fact that I killed someone. I hope that one day Jason and Dianne will forgive me.

Laura Percival.'"

McNab looked up at Ng and Collotti. "Christ, what a bloody waste. The poor thing didn't know that she hadn't killed him. She only intended to help him relax--not kill him. Mind you, we know that because of the autopsy report. In her confused state of mind, without the knowledge that he hadn't drowned, but was poisoned, she obviously blamed herself. Suicide is such a waste of life at any time, but this one is pointless."

Collotti said, "Jason told me that his mother had been a manic-depressive for over twenty years. Since Jason was born, she has literally lived as a recluse and was but a shadow of her former self."

McNab did not reply to Colletti's last statement, immersed in his own thoughts. That remark about her being a shadow of her former self was probably more accurate than he realised. Looking at her, lying in bed, she reminded McNab of an aging

Greta Garbo. It was tragic that she'd so little self esteem, that she decided that death was better than living in a dream world.

Ng asked, "What happens now, sir?"

Andy cleared this throat. "Vincent, handle that vial with care. If I'm not mistaken, it's the same type of vial that was found yesterday in the garden. If it contains remnants of poison hemlock, Lady Laura may have unwittingly killed her husband. She states in this letter that she was advised that the potion was a good relaxant. I think someone talked her into believing that the vial's contents were relatively harmless. It's now up to us to start questioning all the family, friends and associates to see if we can find out something that might point us towards anyone who hated Sir Peter enough to murder him. Unfortunately, there's going to have to be another autopsy, this time on Lady Laura. A handwriting expert can verify that she wrote the note. God, I was thinking that this might be a straightforward case." Andy ran his right hand through his hair. "In answer to your question, our next step is to go over Sir Peter's life, background, business dealings, and friendships. We must find someone with clear motive for murder. Tell me, Vincent, what did we know about Sir Peter before today's information?"

"Well, we know that he had a successful business career, preceding his entry into politics three years ago. He was heavily involved in the local farmer Co-op and, as such, had instigated through government channels an investigation into discrepancies in the Co-op's funds. The Commissioner asked you, as a local resident in the region, to check into possible corruption and report back if you felt the fraud squad should be called in. You did some 'social inquiries' and concluded that the Fraud squad should be called in. They're now investigating the Co-op's books." Vincent paused.

McNab smiled and said, "Good, go on."

"From what we've heard, Sir Peter commanded a powerful presence. He had a strong, dynamic personality and was respected by everyone who knew him. As the grandson of the original founder of the famous Woodburne Winery, he was regarded as the local hierarchy."

McNab nodded at the last comment. "Yes, like Woodburne dominates the local landscape, he did the same. He dominated the local area with his presence as a strong and, as we now learned, an unyielding personality. He was used to having power, money and getting his own way. Dianne told us about her nickname of 'hatchet man', which only emphasises these points. The local gossip will be interesting once the murder story hits the press."

Collotti interrupted McNab. "The rumours are already starting to fly around, sir. I've heard many spiteful remarks about Sir Peter from some of the Co-op members in the pub last night. He wasn't as popular amongst the members as the committee wants everyone to believe. One member said that the majority of the committee were hand-picked 'Yes Men.' No one stayed on the committee long if they disagreed with him."

McNab turned to Collotti. "I'd like you to keep listening to these rumours, Frank. Can you jot down the names of the discontents? I'd like to have a chat with them."

"Consider it done, sir," replied Collotti.

McNab looked over as Sarah escorted Doctor Poulter into the room, then quietly left to return to sit with Joan. The Doctor nodded at McNab.

"What a sorry time this family is having, Inspector."

McNab replied quietly, "Yes, this family has had problems, and will probably have a lot more once the dust settles."

"I presume you wish Sir John Grey to do an autopsy, just in case it's another murder, Inspector? Sorry, I didn't tell you, but Sir John informed me on the phone that Sir Peter's death is now officially murder. He rang me about ten minutes before Detective Sergeant Sedgewick rang to say Lady Laura had been found dead."

"Yes, I'm afraid it will be another job for Sir John Grey. We need to make sure. If it's not murder, then it's simply a rather sad and pointless suicide." He turned to Ng and Collotti and added, "Frank, I'd like you to stay here with Doctor Poulter. Vincent and I will see if we can get any more information from Joan Wilson."

"Yes, sir," replied Collotti, standing tall and straight.

McNab and Ng went downstairs and entered the lounge room just as Sarah was helping Joan Wilson to her feet. Sarah looked up.

"I think Mrs. Wilson should go home and rest."

A quick look at Joan Wilson confirmed to McNab that Sarah was right. It was going to be pointless trying to talk to her further that day. He motioned Sarah closer.

"Yes, you're right, lass," he said in a low voice. "Take her home in the police car, then return here. We have to wait until Doctor Poulter has finished completing his paperwork, and Lady Laura's body has been collected and taken to the city morgue."

"It's sad to think that she is about to end up in the morgue with her husband," whispered Sarah, then turned and went across to Mrs Wilson. "Come on Mrs. Wilson, I'll take you home now. I've phoned your husband. He said that he'll get home to be with you as soon as he can."

Joan Wilson was still wringing her hands on her apron. This time, however, it was not to dry them, but appeared to be an automatic response to stress.

She swayed slightly as Sarah helped her get her bag. She stopped at the front door and looking at Sarah with red, swollen eyes. "Thanks, dear." She then turned back and looked at McNab. "You have all been so kind. It's strange to be saying this at this moment, but I think that Lady Laura has finally found peace. She has been such an unhappy person for years. I felt so sorry for her. We were good friends, you know. Sir Peter probably didn't realise how close we were."

Joan Wilson and Sarah then disappeared through the front door and into the sunshine.

Vincent Ng looked at McNab. "Interesting that she feels that she was closer to Lady Laura than Sir Peter knew eh, boss?"

McNab smiled at Ng. He was glad to think that Ng was feeling more at ease in his company. "Yes, Vincent. I noticed that Joan was implying some sort of secrecy or conspiracy that she and Lady Laura had over Sir Peter. The ladies obviously had an affinity. Let's hope we'll find out more from her tomorrow." What big secret did she share with Lady Laura?

* * *

An hour later, the van from the morgue solemnly drove down the winding drive away from Woodburne, carrying the late Lady Laura's body.

McNab anxiously looked at his watch. "It's nearly four o'clock. Where's Sarah?"

As he spoke, a police car appeared at the gates in the distance. It climbed the winding drive and came to the front steps of Woodburne. McNab, Ng, and Collotti squinted into the afternoon sun. The familiar face of Sarah grinned at them from behind the wheel.

"Sorry I took so long," she called out. "I decided to stay with Joan until her husband arrived from work." She handed over the driver's seat to Collotti.

Ng sat in the front seat, while McNab got into the back with Sarah. Collotti then drove them back to Sunbury Police Station. The plastic evidence bags containing the empty vial, glass and whisky bottle and the apparent suicide letter, were quickly despatched in a car to the forensic laboratories at the city morgue.

It was after six before Sarah drove Andy McNab back towards his property in Gisborne.

"Been quite an eventful day hasn't it?" she stated, her eyes squinting into the sun. "Bloody shame that Lady Laura took her life before finding out the real reason why her husband died. Have you issued orders for the poison to be suppressed from the press in the hope that someone will accidentally let something slip?"

"Yes, however, I don't think that will happen, but you never know. Let's hope we can find out who supplied the vial to her, with such a vague description about the lethal capabilities of the contents. That unknown person may even be our murderer."

"You mean that someone could be manipulating the Percival family and killing them, one by one?"

"Perhaps, lass. We may have a potential serial killer on our hands."

Sarah turned into the gates at the entrance to McNab property. Two sleek, white and curly forms were running towards then, pink tongues hanging out. McNab got out, opened the gate and called out, "Do you mind another bath today, Sarah?"

She laughed. "Not at all! Come on, get in, Snow and White."

McNab closed the gates after Sarah drove through. Snow and White sat panting in the back seat as Sarah drove down the drive, giggling as every few seconds she received either a hot pant or a wet slurp on her neck.

"Heck, do they ever stop licking?"

"Aye, when they're asleep."

As Sarah stopped the car at the front door, Andy suddenly felt awkward again. *Damn, I can't get too close to her. I've always said that I wouldn't get involved with a workmate.* He smiled at her and said, "I guess you don't want to stay long. It's been a long day and it'll possibly be even longer tomorrow. I'll be driving in early tomorrow to the city office to do some paperwork before going to Lady Laura's autopsy at nine. I'd like you to attend with me."

Sarah nodded. "Of course. I'll meet you at the morgue at nine. Better still, I'll meet you in the office. You'll want your usual early morning de-cafe poured for you anyway."

"Talking about de-cafe, would you like a quick cup before you head off?" asked McNab.

"Yes, thanks."

Half an hour later, they were back outside. McNab opened the driver's door for her. She smiled at him as she got in. "Thanks."

"Next time you come here, lass, I'll cook you one of my favourite curries."

"Curry? I thought you Scots are into haggis!"

He laughed at her. "Nothing like a hot meal and a glass of wine between friends, lass."

"Friends, or workmates?" she replied.

"Friends, Sarah. Let's not spoil a good friendship with business."

Sarah started the car and drove off. The dogs had conned another ride to the gate. Andy watched as she stopped, let them out of the car, then opened the gate. The dogs sat watching her drive the car out and close the gate again. Sarah turned and waved at him. He waved back as she drove slowly away. The two white flashes bounded back to the house.

18

"Hmm--I'll need to test the stomach contents with the remnants in the vial that you found next to her body, Andy."

Sir John Grey peered over his half-rimmed glasses at Andy as he spoke. Sarah sat behind the raised viewing area, jotting some thoughts and reactions into her notebook, whilst recording his comments onto her digital recorder. Sir John's assistant quickly started to analyse the specimens.

"How long will that take?" asked McNab.

"Not more than ten minutes, if it's what I suspect Andy," replied Sir John.

"What do you suspect?"

"Probably the same thing that is on your mind, Andy. Poison hemlock! We'll check for that first."

Sarah kept writing.

"Do you think she knew it was poison?" asked Sir John.

"I honestly don't know. Maybe future evidence from other people will tell us," replied McNab.

"Naturally, Andy, you will have to wait for the writing experts to verify that she wrote the note."

"Even if she did write it, we don't know if she wrote it voluntarily," stated McNab.

"Careful, Andy, don't jump to conclusions yet. Lady Laura was a fairly healthy person for her age. By the way, how are those beautiful white beasts of yours?"

Andy laughed. "Still the same. Lovable and playful as ever."

"As wet and sloppy as usual, too," muttered Sarah.

"Pardon, Sergeant?" asked Sir John.

"Sorry, Sir John, just talking to myself," she replied.

Andy winked at her. He hadn't slept very well last night, as dreams and thoughts had kept him awake. A lot of the thoughts were about Sarah. He had been struggling all night to come to terms with these thoughts and feelings and was finding it hard to concentrate on the droning voice of Sir John.

Sir John walked over to where his assistant was peering at the specimens taken from Lady Laura's stomach and from the medicine vial.

"Well, well, well, come and take a Bo-peep, Andy." McNab went across to look. Sir John showed him the first results. "This means that Lady Laura drank whisky that was spiked with poison hemlock, mate. There was no possible way that she wouldn't die!"

"What we need to find out now is if she

instigated this herself, or if in her confused state of mind, she was under the allusion that what she was taking was only a sedative, as she stated in her letter. That's if she wrote the letter," replied McNab.

"Well that's it for now, Andy. You'll have the full written report by tomorrow morning at the latest--maybe even late today with a bit of luck, if the writing experts have finished. Once all this business is over, Andy, you must come over to our place for dinner. Vera has been nagging me that we haven't seen you for a while. It's our turn to cook and entertain. Mind you, we loved that last curry you cooked when we visited last month. Try to surprise Vera for a change and bring someone. It's time you found someone else in your life, mate."

McNab felt a little ill at ease, but feigned cheerfulness when he replied. "Thanks, John. I'll take up your invitation when this investigation is over."

He went over to the basins, took off the plastic apron, overalls and boots that were compulsory attire when standing near to any autopsy. He then took off the latex gloves, washed the powder off his hands, then looked over to Sarah. "Got it all, Sarah?"

"Yes, sir. Everything's recorded."

"Good, then it's time we went back to Sunbury and the murder jigsaw puzzle. Thanks, John, see you soon. Give my love to Vera."

"I will, Andy. Take care," replied Sir John.

As they walked to the entrance, McNab said, "We'll go straight to Sunbury, lass."

"What about your car?"

"I'll collect it when I return to the city."

They got into the police car outside the Morgue.

"How long have you known Sir John Grey?" asked Sarah.

"Since university day's, lass. He was finishing his medical degree when I was doing my arts degree in fine arts and sociology. We were, and still are, both keen on classical music. We used to go to concerts together. Vera was at the same university, doing her music degree. She was a friend of Rhonda's. That's how we met." His voice trailed off. The memories were still painful. He smiled briefly at her and added, "You're one of the few people to hear me call him John and not Sir John, and I know you won't tell anyone. It's hard to keep up the formal protocol between friends."

"Understood, boss!"

"Sarah--I'm sorry. I didn't mean--I mean--I don't know what I mean really. Friends are friends. I usually keep business and my private life separate. John, or should I say Sir John, is probably wondering why I lapsed into calling him John. Then again, he's never asked me about the dogs in the middle of an autopsy before."

McNab was quiet again, staring at the city traffic, as Sarah skilfully negotiated them through the snarl of cars and out onto the toll-way heading towards Sunbury. They were silent for nearly twenty minutes, and then suddenly both talked together in a rush.

"Another nice day, boss."

"Looks like a change coming, lass. Look at those clouds."

There was instant silence, followed by laughter.

"A change? You mean it's going to rain. I put my washing out this morning. Bloody typical of Melbourne's weather," grumbled Sarah.

"Aye, we never know what's going to happen next, do we?" replied McNab.

They were coming near to the Sunbury turn off. Sarah slowed down, put on the left indicator and said, "Well, Sunbury still looks the same as yesterday. I wonder what other surprises we're going to have."

"Aye, I wonder. Sinclair told me earlier this morning that we will have to interview Fredrico Gambello and his father at their vineyard. Apparently, due to the recent hot weather, and rains, they are harvesting some of their vines earlier than expected. I've met Pino. He's the farmer Co-op's secretary. In fact he's the main person who persisted that Sir Peter should organise a Government inquiry."

Ten minutes later, Sarah pulled up in the car park in front of the Sunbury Police station. She pointed to the sturdy figure of Constable Julie Wiseman, disappearing into the front entrance as they closed the car doors. She said in a low voice, " It's only ten in the morning and she's taking a bag of food into the office already."

Julie Wiseman greeted them at reception, and promptly offered some doughnuts to eat.

"No thanks, Julie. We had something to eat, just before we came here," McNab lied, winking at Sarah.

"Thanks, Julie, but I couldn't fit anything else in at the moment," said Sarah.

"That's okay. All the more for lil" old me!" replied Julie, undeterred.

Sergeant Sinclair came in. "'Morning. Another busy day, eh? Do you want someone from uniformed branch to accompany you to the Gambello winery?"

"No, thanks. I know the way. We'd better get going soon. Has Vincent arrived yet?"

"Right here behind you, boss," said Vincent, startling McNab.

The three detectives set off for Gambello Vineyard. The vineyard was on the outskirts of Sunbury. The paddocks of vines stretched out into the distance, down the sloping hill, ending at the railway line. The line was the main country line into

Sunbury that continued on for another one and a half hours, terminating at Bendigo, a large country centre in the north of the state.

The house was big and rambling, with wide, shady veranda's. Large pine trees surrounded the house. The driveway wound around a large fountain, situated near the front door. The fountain's main feature was a statue of a little boy, pissing into the pond surrounding him below.

The trio went to the front door, where McNab lifted the huge brass knocker and dropped it several times, creating a large thud on the thick oak door.

A big, bouncy lady with black hair tied up into a large bun opened the door. She flashed a wide smile, showing two gold-capped teeth. "Allo, you musta be the Inspectore. I'm Ma Gambello. Pleez come in."

She showed them into the front lounge room, where Vincent Ng set up the tape recorder for the interview. Ma Gambello smiled at them.

"I brew the besta coffee. I bring it in."

McNab smiled. He could understand why everyone liked the lady. She exuded warmth and instant friendship.

A minute later, she returned with a large silver service on a tray, complete with coffee pot, milk jug and sugar bowl with silver-clawed tongs and plate of small homemade Italian biscuits, coffee cups, and saucers.

"Self-service, as youz say." She then giggled and added, "Dianne, sheez right. You are a 'spunk', Inspectore, and youz are pretty, Sergeant. Myself--I think youz maka loverly couple!" With that, she left the room.

McNab could feel his face flushing. He kept his head down and avoided looking at Sarah, who was unusually quiet. Finally, he cleared his throat. "Humph! Go and get Fredrico, please Vincent."

Vincent, grinning, quietly left the room.

19

Fredrico Gambello was twenty-five years old. As McNab already knew through yesterday's interviews, he was a friend of Jason and Joe. In fact, he was one of the 'locals', being born, bred, and educated in Sunbury. His deep brown-black eyes stared at McNab. Ng had advised him of his legal rights and now dictated the introductory formalities onto the tape.

"It's Sunday the thirteenth of January. The time's eleven a.m., this interview is being held in the presence of Mr Fredrico Gambello, his solicitor Mr. David Li, Detective Inspector Andy McNab, Detective Sergeant Sarah Sedgewick and Detective Constable Vincent Ng."

"I don't have an alibi, Inspector. Not for the morning that Sir Peter was found dead anyway. I was at home, sick and alone."

The voice was deep and rich. McNab hoped that they did not have another antagonistic interviewee on their hands.

"Yes, your wife Dianne told us yesterday that you were at home alone with a gastric upset. The fact that she also told us that you had kept her awake most of the night before is an alibi for the previous night." McNab then decided to continue using a different tactic. "Did you like Sir Peter?"

Fredrico looked surprised, then bemused and with a slight smile replied, "Like him? He was, after all, my father-in-law. Between us, I got on fairly well with the old sod for Dianne's sake. I can't say I feel any grief at his death. You probably already know that, since we married, Dianne and I have kept fairly distant from the Percival family's inner sanctum."

"Was there a family dispute that caused this distance between Dianne and her family?" asked McNab.

"No, not really what you'd call a dispute. It's simply that her parents didn't really like the fact that their precious daughter was going to marry an Italian. Stupid really, especially as I went to Salesian College with Jason. I went through Melbourne Technical College with Joe Wilson. We graduated in viticulture together. I know Sir Peter was socially friendly with my father Pino, through the farmers Co-op, but it's painfully obvious that neither Sir Peter nor Lady Laura thought my mother or father, were qualified to join their social gatherings." Fredrico scowled, his lips set in a straight line.

"But there was a wedding at Woodburne, with all the trimmings," Andy said. "Your parents were invited surely?"

"Oh, yes. Mother had a wonderful time. The Percival seniors, however, especially Sir Peter, made sure that she was kept in the background, except when the official photos were being taken."

"What about Jason?"

"Hey, Jason loves my Ma, just as much as Joe and everyone else in the district. Ma was born in Italy, and spent most of her life working on her father's vineyard. She met my father when he visited our Italian property to taste and sample the famous wine there. It was love at first sight apparently. They are still wonderful romantics, Pa and Ma. I love them very much and Dianne loves them, too. They are the loving parents to her that Sir Peter and Lady Laura weren't."

"If there was so much underlying friction, why the big wedding?" asked McNab.

"Ah, Inspector, you need to understand what Sir Peter was really like."

"Tell me."

"He was a man who liked to show off his wealth and power over everything and everyone in the district. The wedding was an occasion to show off this power. His beautiful daughter was a secondary consideration, believe me! His speech was almost a 'paid political broadcast'. Still, in spite of all this, Dianne and I had a beaut day with our friends like Jason and Joe and other school friends from Sunbury." Fredrico then added, with a big smile and look of pride, "My mother's English may not be the 'Queen's English' but she more than makes up for that with the absolute and unquestioned love she gives to everyone she meets."

"Fredrico, were you aware that Sir Peter had recently changed his will."

"We know about it now. Earlier this morning, we were meant to attend an official reading of the will, but that was cancelled owing to Lady Laura's death. Jason called in and told us about what he knew this morning. He wanted us to know before it became public knowledge. He's worried that it might put Dianne and me in a bad position."

"Oh, how?"

"You know--wanting the old man dead and all. Truth is nothing could be further from that. I will eventually own this vineyard. I'll also inherit my mother's family vineyard in Italy." Fredrico looked straight into McNab eyes and continued. "Not everyone knows it but, although Pa is a wealthy man, Ma is a multi millionaire in her own right. She's really a 'Countess'. Her title was inherited when her mother died ten years ago."

Lucre isn't a problem with this suspect, McNab thought. *Loathing might be more appropriate though. Did you hate your father-in-law enough to want to kill him?*

Fredrico continued his story. "To be truthful, my family is one of the wealthiest in Italy -- and

Europe for that matter!"

"Your family obviously doesn't bother about using her title then?" asked Sarah.

"Hell, no. She's never been happier since she came to Australia. It's funny, but Sir Peter never knew. For all his snobbery, he would have loved to know that I'm officially a Count. It's a title inherited from my mother's father. What I'm trying to say is that Dianne and I don't need Sir Peter's money. Never did!"

"What do you think about Joe Wilson being included in the new will then?"

"To be honest, Dianne and I were stunned when Jason told us. Jason was surprised, too. None of us knows why. Even Joe can't understand why. It's a mystery to all of us. Maybe one of the older folk may know why. Who knows."

That was an interesting comment. Indeed why? If they knew why, then they might be able to find a more definite suspect. Strange, that here was a family, who had every right to be seen as local royalty or the like, but didn't want the recognition. McNab was beginning to understand why Dianne was happier being part of the Gambello flock.

"Thanks, Fred. That's all for now." With those words, McNab terminated the interview. As they got up to leave, Ma Gambello rushed into the room.

"Pleez don't leave justa yet. Pino wants to see

youz in the wine tasting area before youz go, eh."

She ushered them across to a wooden building, shaped like a huge wine barrel. This building was the place where the tourists and appreciators of good wine came to sample, taste, and eventually buy some wine. The door opened and Pino Gambello motioned them in. He shook hands with McNab.

"I see Isabella has been looking after you. I thought that you might like a short tour of the winemaking procedure. You are just in time to see some of the grapes picked earlier today being crushed. I know you're on duty, but perhaps you may like to sample just a little of the wine, eh? You can also enjoy a small bowl of Ma's famous pasta for lunch. You need a break during the day."

"Well-- I-- ah--" started McNab, then glanced at the eager faces of Sarah and Vincent, realising that he couldn't refuse such an invitation. He gave in. "Well, why not?" He followed Pino Gambello inside with Sarah and Vincent close behind.

20

Pino Gambello was a wonderful host. He showed the three detectives the machines crushing the freshly picked grapes. They were fascinated with the fact that they were actually seeing the vineyard's future Chardonnay being crushed, ready to put into the huge barrels to ferment. Pino chatted about how each vintner kept each vineyards special winemaking process or 'recipe' a closely guarded secret. That way the vineyard would hopefully retain their advantage wine quality and sales over their opposition wineries.

Ma Gambello was true to her word and supplied each of them with a delicious bowl of homemade bolognaise. It was whilst eating his meal that Andy McNab received some important inside information regarding Sir Peter and the Co-op. He had casually asked Pino what his true opinion was of Sir Peter. The reply was unexpected.

"I never liked the man personally. However it was in my best interest to keep on socially friendly terms with him for business reasons and also for Dianne and Frederico's sake."

"Business reasons? What do you mean, Pino?" McNab replied.

"Inspector, there were obvious professional jealousies between us, but I knew that if I became a direct threat to Sir Peter, his business, his politics or his family, he would make my life hell on Earth, you know what I mean?"

"I understand perfectly, Pino. Sir Peter was a man of great influence, wasn't he?"

"That, Inspector, is the biggest understatement that I've heard. I'm just glad that he liked me. Let's leave it at that, shall we?"

"If you like, for the moment."

"Inspector, I need to add one more thing about Sir Peter."

"Oh, what's that?"

"I think that Sir Peter was directly involved in the Co-op's discrepancies!"

McNab nearly choked on the long tube of spaghetti that he was slowly sucking into his mouth. "You what?"

"Unfortunately, like the fraud squad, so far, I have no proof, Inspector."

The large Italian grandfather clock standing in the reception area of the wine tasting, food and entertainment barn struck one, as the three detectives finally left the Gambello Vineyard and waddled to the police car. Vincent started the engine, then turned to McNab.

"That homemade pasta was great. Back to the Sunbury police station, boss?"

"No, not yet. Next stop is the Victoria Bank to see Roger Wilson. Aye lad, that pasta was wonderful. Another recipe I'd like to get my hands on," replied McNab.

"Going to try Italian cooking next? I thought you liked cooking curries?" said Ng.

"Curries? Whatever gave you that impression?" asked McNab trying to look casual.

"Where is the bank, boss?"

21

McNab directed Ng to the bank in Main Street, near the Railway station. They parked in the customer car park at the rear, then walked up the side street to the entrance. McNab had hoped that they would look like ordinary customers. To his dismay, it seemed that everyone inside the bank, customers and staff alike stopped for a second to look and stare at their entrance.

There went the subtle entry!

He walked over to the customer service desk and talked to the girl behind the counter. He felt as though his question may as well have been broadcast through a loudspeaker system, as no one else was talking as he spoke. He could literally feel all the locals' eyes boring into him as he spoke.

"Detective Inspector Andy McNab. Is Mr. Wilson in?"

"Yes, of course, Inspector. Come this way, please." She ushered the detectives through the doorway at the back of the public area.

Roger Wilson got up and walked around from behind his desk to greet them. "Thanks, Agnes.

Good afternoon. Please make yourselves comfortable."

Andy introduced Sarah and Vincent, who sat on either side of Andy, each with notebooks and pens.

"I can't believe that it's only just five days since that dinner at Woodburne, Inspector," said Wilson. He obviously felt that the moment demand that he use Andy's formal title.

McNab replied, "Yes, if feels like months ago to me, Roger. How is Joan today?"

"Much better than yesterday, thanks, Andy. It's been such a shock to both of us. First, Sir Peter's death, then Lady Laura's. As you no doubt realise, the whole town's buzzing with all sorts of gossip today, especially since the news about Lady Laura's death hit the newspapers this morning."

"You knew that Sir Peter had changed his will?" stated McNab.

"Obviously! You've seen a copy of the new will, Andy. It has my signature on it as one of the witnesses. Sir Peter's solicitor was the other signatory."

"What was your first reaction to the new will's contents?

"I was stunned, of course. I found it hard to believe that Sir Peter had actually named my son as the new equal beneficiary. I still don't understand why. Perhaps I can understand why he omitted Dianne. Sir Peter was a patriarchal figurehead,

Andy, and, as such, he didn't believe that women should have careers, wealth, or power in their own right. Women, to Sir Peter, were purely the opposite sex that was born for man to enjoy, for procreation and to be good housewives." Roger Wilson instantly noticed Sarah's horrified reaction and added, "Yes, it's a pretty archaic attitude, Sergeant, I agree, but that's the nature of the beast."

"Do you think Sir Peter chose Joe because of his qualities as a manager?"

Roger Wilson nervously sipped water from a glass on his desk and cleared his throat. "I know what you're inferring. I know he often thought more of Joe than Jason, but I can't believe that Joe got the job because I was Sir Peter's bank manager. There is something that you should know. Joe is not our natural son, Inspector. He's adopted. When we found out that we couldn't have children of our own, Doctor Rose arranged a private adoption."

"Was that legal?" asked Sarah.

"Oh, the paperwork was all perfectly legal. On hindsight, today, I guess we had some mysterious benefactor who helped us through into the fast lane, so to speak. I know that sounds as though we were greedy or something, but Joan and I were so keen to have a child. Unless you've been in the same position, you wouldn't understand."

"Do you know who Joe's real parents are?" asked Ng.

"No, that was part of the adoption laws twenty-three years ago. I know the law's different today. Adopted children can seek out their actual parents."

"Not always successfully," remarked Sarah.

"I know," sighed Wilson, and continued, "If I were in Joe's position, I would want to know about my heritage. He's tried, you know, but without success. The records only show that his mother died in childbirth in Tasmania, and that his father was unknown. Doctor Rose died years ago. The mother's name on the certificate is an alias, which we can't trace. It's as if she didn't exist!"

"What did you really think of Sir Peter and Lady Laura, Roger?" asked McNab.

"Well, let's say I never had a really high opinion of either of them really. I found Sir Peter to be a domineering, stubborn, patriarchal family man, an aggressive businessman and a publicity-seeking politician." He paused. "My, that was quite a mouthful for me. But I needed to say it sooner or later. Lady Laura was, well, simply a beautiful, dumb blond, if I can say that without offending anyone using that euphemism. She was Sir Peter's little attractive lap dog, if you like. Joan could tell you more about that, having been their housekeeper for over twenty years. You know they slept in separate rooms after Jason was born. That's when Lady Laura had her nervous breakdown. Joan was hired as the housekeeper to look after the baby and Dianne. She brought up Jason and Dianne as if they were her own children. Poor Jason and Dianne never knew what their mother was really like."

"Roger, could you get me a copy of Sir Peter's bank accounts? asked McNab.

"You obviously mean to check for regular payments or something like that?" replied Wilson.

"Exactly!" said McNab.

Roger Wilson smiled. "Off the record, Inspector, I know you're not investigating the Co-op corruption thing, but I personally reckon Sir Peter could have been involved."

"Oh, why?"

"Peter Cotti, the Co-op's secretary often hinted so to me. I tend to think he could be right, but there was no proof. I found nothing out of order when I audited the last lot of books anyway. The so-called missing funds were all cash donations from people who wanted to remain anonymous. I think that whoever needed the cash, took full advantage of this," replied Wilson.

McNab's thoughts were instantly racing. *Och, that's interesting. Maybe the Co-op's fund discrepancies and Sir Peter's murder could be linked after all.*

McNab finished the interview, and the detectives left the bank. McNab again felt that everyone seemed to be staring at them as they went out the door. The short drive back to the Sunbury Police Station was in silence. Sarah first spoke.

"Well, it's beginning to look as though Sir Peter didn't have many genuine friends."

"Aye, lass. He wasn't the nice family man that I thought him to be, that's for sure. So far, we seem to be coming up with a lot of dead ends. We need to talk with Peter Cotti. He might be able to give us something of interest. I'd also like to talk to Joan Wilson again. In the meantime, we can start sifting though all that paperwork that we took from Sir Peter's desk."

As Vincent pulled the car up at the station, McNab looked briefly at his watch, then snapped, "Three o'clock already? Let's get inside and start looking at that paperwork."

Two hours later, the three detectives took a short coffee break.

McNab yawned. "Vincent, I'd like you to go back to the city office so that first thing tomorrow morning, you can to go to Sir Peter's old business office and ask a few questions. See if anyone there shows any agro. Get a list of people who were sacked by Sir Peter if you can. Maybe our murderer could be one of his ex employees. We need to make sure."

"I'll leave now, boss. I'll phone you on your mobile if I find anything." With that last statement, Vincent left.

"Now, I think it's time for us to grab some take-away to eat back at my house. We can keep searching through this paperwork back there. These chairs are getting too hard." McNab stopped talking, looked at Sarah, then added, "You don't mind do you? I need a lift back anyway. I thought we could get some of this paperwork done in comfort."

"Heck, why should I mind? I need another doggy bath anyway," she laughed.

22

Snow and White stretched out contentedly on the family room floor, full of not only their own dog food, but also the left over scraps of the large pizzas that McNab and Sedgewick hadn't finished.

"Sir Peter was a real hoarder wasn't he?" remarked Sarah.

Scattered around her, in various piles, were family snap shots, photos of the family and of unknown people.

McNab replied, "That's not unusual. I have a carton full of photos myself, which I keep promising to put into some sort of order and into albums one day. That day never seems to come." He pretended to be reading one of the Percival papers, but his mind was in overdrive.

Why am I defending this man? Is it because I'm frightened that one day I might become like him? Sir Peter was arrogant, domineering, and used to getting his own way. My rank doesn't help matters. I'm expected to put on a veneer of authority and aloofness. Have I spent too much time putting up a private barrier around myself since Rhonda died? Why can't I let her go? Why can't I let her become simply a happy memory and not the ghost who constantly haunts me? When the job requires that we probe into the private life of a victim, I feel vulnerable, too. It's times like this that I realise how little others know about me.

They continued in silence, sifting through the papers and the file that had now become a type of written testimony of Sir Peter's life. The file had been taken from Sir Peter's safe in the presence of Jason, and with his permission. Significantly, Joe had also been present at that time. The only noise was the soft snoring from one of the dogs and the rustle of papers, which seemed to blend in with the Vivaldi CD that McNab had put on.

It was nearly an hour later when McNab straightened up from the coffee table. "Well, well, what have we here?" He was holding a folder of private cheque account statements.

"By the look on your face, you've found something in the Percival closet. Is it one of the skeletons we're hoping to find?"

He grinned back at her. "Sir Peter's cheque account shows a regular monthly payment of one thousand dollars being paid into an account number in the same bank. There's no name. Just the initials LJ."

Sarah looked at the statement in Andy's hand. "LJ? None of our current suspects or local identities has those initials."

"I realise that, Sarah. I wonder if he was being

blackmailed. The payments stopped about a month ago. I'll get Roger Wilson to check the account name for us tomorrow morning, as it's the same bank. Coffee or something stronger?"

"Coffee sounds good."

McNab wandered into the kitchen and put the kettle on. Five minutes later, he returned holding a tray containing two mugs, a small jug of milk, and a plunger of steaming coffee. He put the tray on the coffee table, then went to the bar and poured two small glasses of port. As he handed the port to Sarah, he winked and said, "Just a wee glass to keep the brain oiled, eh?"

"Thanks, boss."

"Hey, we're not on duty at the moment. How about dropping the formalities for the rest of the evening? That's if you don't mind calling me Andy?"

"Heck, boss, I mean, Andy, we've been working together for over two years now. I don't find that a problem." She sipped the port and added, "Hmm, nice. By the way, while you were in the kitchen, I found an old agreement signed by a George Percival and a Paul Petty, dated 1890."

"That must be Sir Peter's grandfather. You're holding some Victorian history in your hand, lass. What's the agreement for?"

"Well it's a fairly simple one. George Percival states that Paul Petty, his vintner, would receive part of the profits from the crops each year. The attached recipe is one made by Petty."

"According to what Pino told us at lunch today, those recipes are highly prized. I'll get Roger Wilson to look through the bank files to see how long payments were paid to the Petty family. Tomorrow, you can go to the local council chambers and look through the rate payers list to see if any Petty's are still living in the district."

"Andy, do you think that this contract has become a dispute between the current living members of the families?"

"Perhaps. Pino also hinted that Sir Peter enjoyed using his influence and casting vote when the Co-op had locked disputes. Apparently, nearly every time, his casting vote was the one that passed a motion in favour of the wineries over the other farming industries in the district. Now, Sir Peter's apparent power as the local 'Cock of the Walk' has made all his family and so called friends close ranks like 'Birds of a feather'. It's three days since he died, and we've nothing concrete, except that he was killed by a deadly poison."

Sarah picked up a photograph of a tiny baby. There was no name on the back. "What a lovely baby. I wonder who it is. All the photos of Jason and Dianne are fully labelled with names and dates. This one's only got a date, February 8th, 1973, Hobart. It doesn't look like his hand writing either."

Andy looked at the photo. "All babies look the same to me."

"Oh, how can you say that? Hey, didn't Roger Wilson say that Joe came from Tasmania? He was born twenty three years ago, so that makes it 1972."

"Best person to ask about that photo will be Joan, lass. You're right though, it could be a baby photo of Joe. Why would Sir Peter have that in his private collection of memorabilia? You're right about the handwriting, too. It looks like it's written by a left handed person as it slopes backwards."

The fax machine at the other end of the living room bounced into life.

"Let's hope that's the final autopsy report," muttered McNab. He walked over to the machine, then impatiently tapped his fingers on the table as he waited for the transmission to be completed. "We've got a double murder!"

"What? What about the handwriting?"

"The poison hemlock was apparently mixed or made the same way as the stuff that killed Sir Peter. Lady Laura didn't write the so-called suicide letter either. Sir John Grey had two experts look at the writing and both agree that although the letter was a clever imitation of her writing, a left hand wrote it. Lady Laura was right handed. Hell, I'd better phone Sergeant Sinclair and ask him to get an officer out to Woodburne and to Gambello to keep an eye on Jason and Dianne. If it's a serial killer, we don't want them to be the next victims."

"I don't think any of our current suspects are left handed, Andy. Hell, this is turning into a nightmare. Do you think we should get the writing on this baby photo checked against the letter found with Lady Laura?"

"Aye, first thing in the morning. I'll request a handwriting expert to come to Sunbury. We'll get samples of handwriting from everyone that we've talked to so far. You never know."

McNab quickly made the call to Sinclair at his home, then left his request for a handwriting expert. He sighed after he hung up. "Well that's taken care of. Poor old Dennis, I woke him up. Do you know it's midnight! It's too late for you to drive back tonight and then rush back early tomorrow, lass. It's going to be a long, busy day. Why don't you bunk down here?" He suddenly felt awkward. "You can sleep in the spare room on the fold-out couch. I'll get some sheets and a blanket."

Sarah blushed. "Let's organise the sleeping arrangements after we get some fresh air outside."

"Why not? The dogs need a run anyway," he smiled.

They went out onto the back veranda and watched together as the two white, curly dogs flashed around the home paddock at the back of the house. They ran gracefully, like long-coated greyhounds, the full moon reflecting off their coats.

"It's beautiful here, Andy. So peaceful compared to my little balcony in the city."

Andy looked at Sarah and realised that it he was becoming more deeply attached to her, perhaps more deeply than he had intended to be, especially with a workmate.

Will I never love anyone else? I must let go my obsession with Rhonda. If only I could finish that portrait of her. Perhaps that what is holding me back? Hell, I think I'm falling in love with Sarah!

Sarah also appeared to be lost in thought, and Andy finally said, "A penny for your thoughts?

"Pardon? Oh, I'm sorry, Andy. I don't know if I should really tell you what my thoughts are. You might think they're wicked."

McNab laughed, then stopped, his head bowed slightly like a schoolboy, confused and unsure of himself.

"Andy, I--I" She choked on her words, then walked over to him and held his face in her hands.

Her body was suddenly against his, and Andy held her firmly as he kissed her. He smiled at her as she stepped back. His voice was husky, as he called to the dogs, and said, "It's time we went inside."

BOOK THREE
Bird's-eye-View

23

Sarah looked at her watch. It was six-thirty and the sun was creeping up over the nearby hills. The door opened, and McNab entered, holding a hot cup of coffee.

"Sorry, I should have knocked, lass. This will brush the cobwebs away anyway. Breakfast is ready. It's only cereal and toast, I'm afraid. By the way, is that fold-out bed comfortable? Did you manage to sleep?"

"Well, let's say I slept like a log. Sorry, Andy, yes it's very comfortable, thanks. Can I use the bathroom for a shower before I eat?"

"Of course, I'll get a towel for you. I'll shower in my en-suite, then we can have breakfast together and talk tactics for today."

McNab was standing in the kitchen pouring some orange juice when she joined him. She looked across at him as they sat opposite each other at the table in the family room, eating cereal and toast.

She pointed at Rhonda's portrait and said, "I can't see anything wrong with the eyes. It's a beautiful painting."

"When I work out what's missing in the eyes, lass, I'll be able to finish it. Now, let's discuss today's tactics."

His face suddenly looked serious. It was time to get back to reality, and work with her. His deep Scottish lilt filled the room as he went through the list of things that needed to be done that day.

"First thing, we'll go to the Sunbury Police station. We need to keep Sinclair up to date with what is happening. Secondly, while you're checking the council records for the name of Petty in the district, I'll go and to talk to Peter Cotti, the Co-op's secretary."

"He has a record?"

"Yes, I think he does. I found a note last night that Sir Peter had scribbled about him having a record. I presume that he meant a police record."

"Another suspect?"

"Perhaps--we also need to have a quick chat with Joan Wilson. You can photocopy the baby photo."

"Yes, boss. Maybe she'll identify it for us."

"Possibly. Thirdly, we--"

Sarah interrupted. "She might finally come forward with some of the family secrets. That's if she knows any."

"Hmmm, perhaps. Thirdly, we need to find out who LJ is and talk to them. With a bit of luck, and we need luck at this stage, Vincent might find out something from Sir Peter's ex-workmates."

They had finished eating. It was time to go. The dogs were first to get into the car, sitting happily in the back seat, tongues hanging out. Sarah took the wheel and drove to the gate. McNab got out of the car and opened the gate for Sarah to drive through. He then let the dogs out of the back and sent them inside the gate, before closing it behind him. The dogs happily ran off to the shady veranda.

McNab and Sedgewick were silent during the twenty-minute drive south to Sunbury. McNab kept trying to analyse, not only the task ahead of them that day, but also his private feelings for Sarah.

What if our relationship develops any further? How can we keep our work life and private life separate? Och, why am I churning this over, again and again? Why is Rhonda still invading my daily thoughts?

His thoughts were jolted back to reality when a car's horn tooted them as they entered the Sunbury Police station car park. It was Sergeant Sinclair following them into the park.

24

Sergeant Sinclair walked to the front entrance with them and told them what he had done so far that day. "I've sent out two officers, one to Woodburne and one to Gambello as you requested, sir. Hell, this is a real mess of a case, isn't it? Two murders in two days! Sunbury is normally a quiet spot."

"Yes, it is a mess at the moment, Dennis. Hopefully it won't be for long. I wonder if you could check up on Peter Cotti for me. I found this note, amongst Sir Peter's personal papers last night. It mentions his name and next to it is written the words record and file."

Sinclair nodded at McNab. "I'll get a print out for your files, but I can briefly tell you the story. Peter Cotti was convicted of a culpable drink-driving incident ten years ago, for which he was given a two-year prison sentence. The driver and passenger of the other car were killed. Apparently, Cotti drove onto the wrong side of the road and they hit, head on. It was a foggy night. He had a blood alcohol level of 0.12. He pleaded guilty and showed remorse. That's why he only got two years,

I guess. He got out on parole nine months later. He'd learned short hand and typing in prison. He's not a bad guy really. Just bloody stupid at the time, driving when he was drunk. He belongs to AA and has a model citizen ever since."

McNab nodded back at Sinclair. "Thanks. I'll still need to talk to him. He's secretary of the Co-op and, as such, was involved closely with Sir Peter. Frank Collotti said that he's heard that Cotti has been spreading rumours about Sir Peter and the missing funds."

"Yes, he told me." Sinclair grinned, then added, "I'll get that print-out of his record from the computer for you now. Won't be long."

McNab wasn't idle during the ten minutes Sinclair was absent from the room. He phoned Roger Wilson, asking him to try and find out the name that belonged to the initials LJ. He also asked if he could arrange a check of the archived files of the Victoria bank. He hoped that such a search might locate the payments made from the Woodburne winery to the Pettys'. He asked to know if the payments were still being made, and if not, why not. Roger Wilson promised to be as quick as possible. McNab gave Wilson his mobile number to contact as soon as he had any results.

Wilson concluded their conversation by saying, "By the way, Andy, err Inspector, I thought that you might like to know that Sir Peter and Lady

Laura's joint funeral service and burial will be held tomorrow morning, Tuesday the fifteenth. It's meant to be a private one with family and immediate friends only. I think there will be some representative from Parliament, too. Members of his party will be there of course, as well as the opposition. Whatever some people may think of him, he was a highly respected businessman and parliamentarian."

"What time is the funeral, Roger?"

"Midday, at the O'Reilly Funeral Parlour. The service will be followed with a private burial at the Sunbury Cemetery."

"Thanks, Roger. Speak to you later."

McNab hung up the phone as Sinclair returned with the copy of Cotti's file, which he handed to McNab. "Do you know the funeral's tomorrow morning, sir?"

"Yes, thanks. We'll attend, but stay in the background of course," replied McNab.

Julie Wiseman entered. "The hand writing expert has arrived, sir. I've lodged him in the spare office, complete with the writing samples of Joe Wilson, Dianne and Fredrico Gambello, Joan Wilson, and Jason Percival, which we retrieved from their original handwritten statements."

"Thanks, Julie," McNab replied. *Good, Sinclair runs a tight ship here. I can rely upon his team for a solid back up. I need all the help I can get now.* "Dennis, let me know if the expert finds out anything important will you?"

"Consider it done, sir."

"We'll see you later in the day, Dennis. Contact me on my mobile number, in case anything crops up."

With that, McNab whisked Sarah out of the police station and got into their unmarked police car.

"Right, Sarah, first stop is the council chambers. I'll leave you there, while I go and talk to Cotti."

25

They stopped outside the front of the Sunbury Council offices, which was almost diagonally opposite the Police station. McNab was at the wheel. He waited for Sarah to get out, then said, "Give me a ring on your mobile when you're ready to be collected. We'll then go and visit Joan Wilson at Woodburne."

"Right, boss, see you later," she replied and walked towards the entrance.

The receptionist looked over her half-framed glasses at her. "Can I help you?"

"Yes, I'm Detective Sergeant Sedgewick. I'd like to check the rate payer's lists for the district if I may."

"Certainly. Come this way. I'll introduce you to the rates officer."

She took Sarah into the office area located behind the public access area. It was the usual public service "rabbit warren", with small but efficient offices lining the corridor. At the far end of the corridor, the receptionist opened the door and showed her in. A tall, skinny young man of about twenty stood up, quickly swallowing his last mouthful of breakfast--the local takeaway hamburger. The receptionist introduced Sarah, then returned to her desk.

"What info do you want, love?" he asked.

She replied, "We need to know about any people with the surname of Petty, past and present in Sunbury. I'd appreciate it if you could start in the old files, if you can access them, dating back to 1890, starting with the name Paul Petty."

"That'll be in the old dusty boxes out the back. Hope you don't mind spiders. Ha, ha. Just kidding. The files are kept in a compacting file section containing the old shire's archives. The local Historical Society cleaned them up recently when they were writing up the history of this area."

She followed him down the passage to another office. Inside was a huge mobile compacting file. He went to the area marked "P-S" and opened it up, making a passageway to walk through with files from floor to ceiling on either side. He moved down to the area labelled 'P' and finally pulled out a folder, which he handed to her. They sat at a table next to the filing system and opened the file.

The file covered the years of the beginning of the settlement, form 1851, the year the village was surveyed, to the year of Federation, 1901. It covered names of the first settlers and landowners of the Sunbury district.

Only one name listed under Petty-- Paul Petty,

who owned the property next door to Woodburne. The Rates Officer delved through the filing system and returned with files covering the years 1902 to 1910, 1911 to 1920, then 1921 through 1950 and finally 1951 to the present.

Half an hour later, they had discovered some interesting information for Sarah's notebook. When Paul Petty had died in 1904, his son, Arthur Petty had taken over the land title. The title then passed on to his son Lyle Petty in 1950, when he was twenty years old, According to the records, he still lived at the farm, on his own. Sarah noted on her pad that he would be now in his seventies.

"Sergeant, there's another Petty living in the district now. His name is Arnold Petty. Don't know if he's a relo, but..."

"Thanks, I'll need his address and details, too. Could you get me a photocopy of each of these pages for me?"

"No worries, Sarge." He disappeared, leaving her sitting alone in the slightly stuffy archive room.

26

Cotti's eyes glowered as he spoke. "Oh, yes, when Sir Peter found out about my prison record, he tried to get me booted off the committee of the Farmers' Co-op during the last meeting. He didn't succeed. As you know, I'm still Secretary."

"How did he try to get you removed from the Committee?"

"Oh the usual veiled threats, like reminding me that "Once an Alcoholic, always an Alcoholic" inferring that I wasn't fit or reliable for the job. I countered his claims with a letter from the local AA group that confirmed that I was now sober, and a dedicated, committed member of the AA. You see, Inspector, I agree that I'll always be an alcoholic. That's what we are taught by the AA counsellors. Alcoholism is not curable. It's only controllable by permanent abstinence. I know the score. One sip and I'm off my face and back in the gutter! There was no logical reason why I couldn't keep my position as Secretary, as long as I remained sober. The other Committee members and general members outvoted Sir Peter's motion of 'no confidence', so it was as simple as that."

"Do you hate him for what he tried to do to you?"

"Inspector, I could lie through my teeth and say no, but that's not my philosophy these days. The fact is, I hated his guts and I'm glad he's dead. But I didn't kill him."

"Where were you between six in the evening and midnight on Friday the eleventh of January Peter?"

"Don't worry, Inspector, I have an alibi. I was conducting the local school orchestra from seven-thirty to eleven-thirty. From seven to seven-thirty, I was helping the kids tune their instruments, and from eleven thirty until around one in the morning, I joined the kids and their parents in supper and soft drinks in the local hall where the concert was performed."

Bang goes another suspect!

"I'll need you to sign your written statement, Peter."

"Of course, no worries, mate."

"Just one more question, off the record, Peter?"

"Fire away, Inspector."

"How sure are you that Sir Peter was involved in the Co-op's fund discrepancies?"

"Oh, I'm very sure, mate. Only problem I have, like others in the Co-op who have the same suspicions, there's no proof. It's impossible to trace where the cash donations were actually given, or whose hands it passed through, as you know. Only way I know would have been to take serial numbers or somethin' like that, eh? The other problem was, and still is, the people who donated the large amounts of the alleged cash, didn't want the authorities to know."

"Oh? Why?"

"Simply the fact that the cash they donated had not been declared to the taxman, you understand?"

McNab was satisfied that he would not learn anything more from Peter Cotti at that point. He made a mental note to check with members of the Fraud Squad who were officially investigating the corruption inquiry, with the hopes that they could get some important information from Cotti.

He left Cotti at the Co-op office, and once outside, rang Sarah on his mobile to see if she was ready to be collected from the Council Offices.

Sarah laughed. "Hi, I've been outside for only a few minutes. I was just about to phone you."

Five minutes later, McNab pulled up, and she jumped into the passenger seat, clutching the file holding the photocopies of the archive files that related to the Petty families.

"So, how many Petty's did you find?" he asked.

"Only two. One is Arnold Petty and the other is Lyle Petty. According to the records, Lyle Petty looks like the grandson of Paul Petty. The records don't show if Arnold Petty is related. We'll have to check them both out, of course. How did you go with Peter Cotti?"

"Drew a blank, as far as suspects go, but it was still an interesting talk, lass. Basically, Sir Peter found out about his prison record and tried to have him dumped off the Co-op committee. However in the end, Cotti had the support of the majority of the members and the committee to stay on, so end of story."

"I bet Sir Peter hated that," remarked Sarah.

McNab continued. "Cotti indicated that he felt Sir Peter was involved with the missing funds fraud. But he reckons there's no proof. I'm going to ask the Fraud Squad to put some more pressure on Cotti. Even if they can't get proof against Sir Peter, I reckon they might turn up a few bad eggs in regard to tax evasion! The large donors didn't want receipts. You know Sarah, I think that Peter Cotti was too close to finding out the truth, and that's why Sir Peter tried the 'no-confidence' motion to get rid of him."

"But the motion was defeated."

"Yes, but that meeting was only a week before Sir Peter was murdered. I doubt if Sir Peter had enough time to launch any other plan to rid the Co-op of Cotti before he was killed."

"Do you think the murderer might be someone involved in the Co-op?"

"I don't know, Sarah. The trouble is there's no evidence to prove the theory. We need hard facts."

"Boss, perhaps we're looking in the wrong direction."

"What do you have in mind? I'm open to any new suggestions, lass."

"The medical vials weren't labelled, which means that the poison wasn't obtained legally, as we know. Yet, whoever extracted the poison from the Hemlock plant must have some sort of herbal knowledge, or grow herbs. So maybe we should be looking through any herbalists in the district."

"That's already been thought of, lass. Collotti followed on from Vincent's suggestion about the wide use of herbs. He's been running a check with Natural therapists and herbalists in the district. Unfortunately, as he found out, lots of people grow their own herbs, in their own back yards, on the kitchen ledge, or even in glass houses. We'd have to do a house to house search of every house in Sunbury, which as an impossible task, given our resources." He smiled at the look of disappointment on Sarah's face, and added, "It was a good idea, lass, but the herb trail would be like looking for a needle in a haystack. Now it's time to talk to Joan Wilson again."

McNab pulled out onto the main road again and headed towards Woodburne.

27

The hands-free kit for McNab's mobile started to ring. After the third ring, McNab answered the call by talking clearly, so the mike situated near his head at the top of the driver's window could relay his voice.

"McNab speaking."

The speaker was clear. "Hello, it's Roger Wilson. I have the information you wanted."

"Good, go ahead. Sarah is with me, her pen poised."

"Well, first of all, the name for Account number 055 142 62717 is Lola Jones. Her address is 42 Crescent Street St., Kilda. Secondly, looking back through the archives, the city office located the payment of royalty monies, also paid each month, from George Percival to Paul Petty. After their deaths, George Percival's son Graham continued the payments to Paul's son Arthur Petty."

"I'll ask the obvious question, Roger. Are payments still being made?" asked McNab.

"Well, the interesting thing is that payments continued to Lyle Petty after his father died. When Graham Percival died, Sir Peter retired from his

136

business and took over the Vineyard. He immediately sent a letter to us with a copy of the letter that he sent to Lyle Petty, stopping the payments. I remember asking him why at the time. His answer was abrupt. He said the agreement was between the two grandfathers only. There was simply no agreement between himself and Lyle, and he never intended to have one. I felt so sorry for Lyle when Sir Peter defeated Lyle's court challenge."

"Thanks for the info, Roger. Could you fax a copy to the letters and you information to my attention to the Sunbury Police station?"

"Of course, I'll do it straight away. I'll see you tomorrow morning at O'Reilly's funeral Parlour."

"Aye. Speak to you then. Bye." McNab ended the call. "We've got a clearer picture of Sir Peter. It looks like he wasn't willing to part with any of his profits. What a greedy sod, especially as it wasn't his wine recipe or to be more correct, as Pino explained to us, his wine process." He paused, then muttered, "Bastard!"

"Who's a bastard?" asked Sarah, looking at him in surprise.

"Och, nothing, lass," he replied, embarrassed. He stroked his moustache. *Careful Andy, you're starting to mumble your thoughts out aloud.*

He turned into the entrance of Woodburne and drove slowly up the curved driveway to the mansion. Joan Wilson was waiting anxiously for them on the front veranda.

"Hello, Joan. I know we should have phoned you and told you we were coming to see you but --"

McNab quickly realised that her agitated state was not the result of their unexpected arrival. He could hear raised voices coming from inside the mansion.

"I'm so glad you're here, both of you. They've been shouting at each other for ages. It's terrible. They're such good friends. It's all because of the letter and the photo."

"Hold on, Joan, let's go inside and we'll try and calm things down."

They hurried inside. In the billiard room, Jason Percival and Joe Wilson were obviously having a very intense argument. McNab heard Joe's voice as they entered.

"If you'd only shut up and listen for a moment, you little prick, you'd realise I knew as little as you did!"

Jason replied, "It's a lie, a bloody lie! It's not true--is it?"

They both stopped, suddenly aware that they weren't alone. The young constable, assigned to watch over Jason, rushed up to McNab.

"Mrs Wilson refused my help, sir, but I was going to interfere if it became physical."

McNab said quietly, "It's okay, Constable. Morning, Jason, Joe. Joan mentioned a letter and a photo. Would one of you like to tell us what this is all about?"

Jason slumped into a chair. Joe sat nearby, then held up a piece of paper and a photo towards McNab. "Look at this, Inspector. I got this in the mail this morning."

McNab took the letter and photo. "Well, well, well. Look, Sarah, it's a copy of the same photo that you found last night."

Sarah said quietly, "It also looks like the same handwriting on the letter, boss"

The letter was written in a backward slope. Even to the untrained eyes, it looked the same as the writing on the back of the photo that Sarah had found in Sir Peter's file. That photo was still in McNab's breast pocket.

"What does the letter say?" asked Joan.

"Go ahead, read it, everyone will know eventually. There's few secrets around this community," sighed Jason, then added, "Joe's right, neither of us knew about this until now." Jason looked at Joe. "I'm sorry, mate. I guess I'm only angry that we never knew!"

McNab read the short letter out aloud.

Joe,

Have a good look at this photo. It's a photo of you as a baby. I'll have to tell you now. It's a photo of Sir Peter

Percival's eldest son. I told him about you last month. He didn't know until then. Quite a shock, isn't it? Joan doesn't know about who you are. He changed his will for you. I'll expect you to reward me or you'll be sorry.

Your Benefactor.

There were a few moments of silence. Joan gasped and Joe jumped up and ushered her to a chair. "For God's sake, mum, don't faint again."

She took a deep breath. "It's all right, I won't faint. It's just that it's such a shock. If it's true, who was your mother then? We know that that her name on your birth certificate is not her real name. Oh, God, this person's threatened you."

"It's okay, mum. You told me that I was adopted years ago. I've had the police guarding me since last night, thanks to the Inspector here. As far as I'm concerned, you will always be my mum!"

Joan burst into tears.

"Oh, Christ!" muttered McNab.

Sarah went over to Joan and put a hand on her shoulder. "Joan? How about we organise some coffee for everyone?

McNab thought, *right, let's get some sanity around here.*

Five minutes later, the four of them sat around the kitchen table. McNab was asking the questions. "None of you knew?"

Everyone shook their heads in response. McNab continued.

140

"You know, I'm angry with myself. As an artist, and as a detective, I'm trained to observe, to observe people in particular. When I interviewed you the other day, Joe, I looked straight into your eyes. You see, I believe that eyes tell a lot about a person, including fear, anger, or sadness. Some say that eyes are the windows to the soul. Joe, you've got your father's spirit, lad. I should've seen that then. I was too intent on asking questions."

Joan stood up and said tearfully, "Joe, you shouldn't be arguing with Jason. After all, you've been the best of friends all your lives. Life is for the living, not for the dead."

"She's right. We need to track down this person before they try to hurt someone else," remarked McNab.

With that last remark, McNab and Sedgewick took their leave.

"Well, Sarah, now we know the big family secret, but we still don't know who the mystery writer is. I'm sure it's the murderer."

"A serial killer?"

"Aye, lass. We've appointments to see Arnold Petty at two, then Lyle Petty around two-thirty. We've time to grab a quick bite at the sandwich bar next to the Station Pub. Dennis reckons they make great sandwiches and good takeaway coffee. You're hungry, aren't you?"

"I'm starving," she replied.

"Good. Nothing like food to help us think."

Sarah started the engine and headed the car down the drive, away from Woodburne.

28

Fifteen minutes later, McNab and Sedgewick were sitting at one of the tables set outside the gourmet sandwich café. They were protected from the hot sun by one of the many trees that were planted around the main shopping streets of the township.

"Hmm, this is just what I need," mumbled Sarah, in between mouthfuls of the large, salad sandwich.

Andy had already finished and was sipping his cappuccino. "Well, lass, as least we now know why Joe was named as a beneficiary in the new will."

"Yes, but who's been sending these notes and photos to members of the family, boss?"

"A left-handed person, for one thing. So far, our original suspects--Joe, Jason, and Dianne--are all right-handed, which pushes them to the back of the queue somewhat. It was obviously a big shock to Joe, Jason, and Joan learning that Joe is Sir Peter's illegitimate, eldest son."

"Well, sir, we still have the Petty's and Lola Jones on the list."

"Aye. I think that--" He stopped when his

mobile started to ring. "McNab speaking. Hmmm? Looks like another skeleton in Sir Peter's closet. Good work, Vincent. We got Lola's name and address from the bank. It'll be interesting to hear what she knows about the Percival family. Sarah and I are just about to go and see Arthur Petty and Lyle Petty. I'll ring you when we've finished. In the meantime, I'd like you to go you see Lola Jones. We can meet back at the city office later this afternoon to compare notes." McNab ended the call, looked across at Sarah and smiled. "Let's get moving, lass. I want to know what the Petty family know about the Percival family."

As Sarah drove the car to the address of Arthur Petty, McNab updated her with the information that Vincent had told him.

"Vincent said that Sir Peter wasn't particularly liked by anyone who worked with him. If we followed up all of these people, we'd be interviewing for weeks. The main piece of info that several of the management talked about, was the 'bit of fluff' or 'other woman' that Sir Peter had on the side--Lola Jones."

"She's the LJ whom Sir Peter was sending money to."

"Yes. The relationship has been going on for years apparently. Goodness knows if Lady Laura knew about it. We'll never know that now she's dead."

Arnold Petty lived in one of the local retirement villages neat little units. Andy and Sarah walked down the neatly trimmed lawn and garden beds that bordered the driveway that wound around each unit. McNab rang the bell at number five. A grey-haired man in his seventies opened the door. He leaned on a walking frame.

"Who are you?" he asked in a gravely voice.

"I'm Detective Inspector Any McNab and this is Detective Sergeant Sarah Sedgewick. We simply need to know if you are related to a Mr Paul Petty, who owned a vineyard in Sunbury at the start of this century."

"These questions, they are to do with the murder, no?" asked Arnold Petty.

McNab noted the European accent. "In an indirect way, yes, Mr Petty. We need to contact Paul Petty's ancestors regarding an agreement that he had with Sir Peter Percival's grandfather, George Percival."

Arnold Petty laughed. "I wish to be a help to the policia, Inspectore, but I cannot do. My real name is Arnold Petrovski. I changed it by what you call the poll deed. Is that what you call it?"

"Deed poll?" prompted Sarah.

"Yes, deed poll in England in nineteen forty-five, after the war. You know the war? I was a Polish man and I wanted to forget, you understand. So I become Arnold Petty. A good English name, no?"

"Yes it is. I'm sorry that we disturbed you," replied McNab.

"Oh, no worry, young man. I need to move my legs, you know. Good exercise to walk to door, no?"

"Yes, it is," smiled Sarah and added, "Thanks for your help, sir."

They walked in silence back to the car.

"Lyle Petty, here we come," muttered McNab.

29

As McNab and Sedgewick were talking to Arthur Petty, Vincent Ng pulled his car up near the front of a luxurious block of flats located in the bay side suburb of St Kilda.

Ng pressed the security bell next to number thirteen. A honey sweet voice came through the intercom.

"You must be the police. I can see you on my monitor. Come in when I press the door release button, young man. I'll be waiting at my front door for you."

There was a buzz and a click as the lock on the main door was released. Ng entered and went to the lifts opposite the entrance. As he exited the lift at the first floor, the first thing he was aware of was some soft music coming from his left. The door to flat thirteen was in that direction. Ng straightened his necktie for the third time and strode purposefully towards the slim lady dressed in a bright red body suit, standing outside number thirteen.

She wore light make-up that had been expertly applied; her long blond hair draped over each shoulder.

"Come in, young man. You must be Detective Constable Vincent Ng."

"That's correct," replied Ng. "Miss Jones, I've come to ask you about the money that Sir Peter Percival paid regularly into your private account, once a month over the past twenty years."

"Money from Sir Peter? What do you mean?

She had turned pale. Trembling fingers fumbled with a box of cigarettes. She took one and lit it. She started to perspire.

Ng opened the folder that he had brought with him and handed her a copy of the account balance sheet that Roger Wilson had faxed to him in the city office, prior to driving to St Kilda. "We know that this account is yours. We also know that one thousand dollars was paid into it each month by a personal cheque of Sir Peter's. Were the payments for services rendered? Or were they to keep you quiet?"

Lola puffed energetically on her cigarette several times, then stubbed it out. She looked directly at Ng. "I'd given up smoking, believe it or not--I started again when I heard about Pete. It was an awful shock. Yes, we were friends. But not the sort of friends you're thinking about, young man. He felt he could talk to me. He was so generous. The money was to help me pay my rent, that's all."

"Come on, Lola, I'm not stupid. Some of Sir

Peter's business acquaintances reckon that he's visited you for years. You obviously didn't just hold hands when he stayed overnight."

Her face was white as she fumbled for another cigarette. "Okay, I'll tell you the truth. After all, I didn't murder him or anything. Mind you, there were quite a few times that I felt like it. He was a bastard sometimes, and wonderful other times. He had a bad temper and he used to drink too much. But he never hurt me physically. I felt sorry for Laura."

"Oh?"

"Don't look so surprised, young man. Laura and I went to school together."

"What?"

"Ah, that's something that his workmates didn't know. When we left, we both went to modelling school in the city together. Laura could have gone far. Instead, she married Pete. That was before he became a Member of Parliament and was knighted. She was rich and beautiful and didn't need to work for a living as I had to. She was adored by the society set. She was a virgin when Pete married her. Dianne was a honeymoon baby." She stopped and looked at Ng, sighed, then leant back in her chair and continued. "Hell, I may as tell you the rest. You're going to find out sooner or later, especially with the new will's contents."

"Please go on, Miss Jones," prompted Ng.

Although he was taking notes, he had his small recorder taping their conversation, sitting on the coffee table.

"I knew about his so-called dubious business dealings in the Co-op. He got where he was in the business world by being a domineering, egotistical bastard. It was as simple as that. Unknown to Pete, my sister became pregnant by him. That was around the time he proposed to Laura. He was always a bit of a lady's man. Anyway, my brother, who was the head of our family, was horrified. You know the usual thing at the time. He sent Celia off overseas. The baby would be adopted. She could then officially return home after her so-called overseas trip, and no one would know."

"So the payments were to keep you quiet?"

"No! As I've already said, the payments were to help me pay the rent. You need to hear the rest of my story, young man. Don't be so impatient."

"I'm sorry, please continue."

"Well, I put a spanner in the works, I guess. You see, my sister and the baby died. My brother wouldn't even tell me where she was buried. Life was terrible at the farm. I was treated like a slave. Finally, he became abusive and told me to leave. I did just that. I left that day, taking everything, and settled in St. Kilda with another model, who I knew from the modelling school days. I had to get money to live. I changed my name, then worked as an escort in Jane's agency."

"You mean you became a prostitute."

"I prefer to call myself an escort, young man. Anyway, a few years later, I met Pete at a cocktail party in the city. Even though I'd changed my hair colour and name, he recognised me straight away. Laura had suffered a nervous breakdown. She was confused, upset, and well, needed female companionship. Like me, he only knew the 'official' story that my brother had reported to everyone, that Celia had died whilst overseas. It was only about a month ago that my brother tried to blackmail Pete into giving him money. He threatened to expose the fact that Celia had his baby. He said that the boy had lived and had been adopted. It sounded fantastic, but we found out that it was the truth. Pete wouldn't be threatened; instead he changed his will to include Joe as one of the rightful heirs. I've got a nephew, and I don't know him." Tears started to well up in her eyes and spill freely down her cheeks as she added, "I'm going to get to know him, before it's too late."

"Why did you change your name?"

"I told you! It was a chance to start a new life away from my domineering brother."

Ng noticed a photo of a beautiful young woman, with wavy brunette hair and deep blue eyes, in an elegant frame, sitting on the coffee table. "Is this a photo of your sister?"

"Yes."

"Can I borrow it? I promise it will be taken care of. I'll return it as soon as I can. I think my boss would like to see it."

"Ok, as long as you take care of it, young man."

"I promise. As Lola Jones isn't your real name, I need to know your true one."

"Lynda--Lynda Petty."

BOOK FOUR
To show the White Feather

30

McNab and Sedgewick drove through the entrance of the Petty property that adjoined Woodburne.

"What a shame this property is falling into disrepair. The vines don't look as well kept as those in Woodburne, sir."

"No, it doesn't. According to the copies of the titles, Lyle Petty took over the vineyard in nineteen-fifty, when his father died. He would have been around twenty. This makes him about sixty-seven years old. It would be too much for an ageing person to work single-handed. I can't see anyone working here today anyway.

"The vines are full of ripe grapes that, even to untrained eye, need picking," remarked Sarah.

"Aye, you're right, lass, and as we now know, he's not getting the financial support through Woodburne royalty payments now either."

Sarah had stopped the car near the front door.

The two of them got out and walked up the veranda steps. McNab rang the bell and waited a few minutes before he rang it again. There was still no answer. "Damn it. He should be here." He rang Petty's phone on his mobile. "Damn! According to the message on his answering machine, he had to see his specialist this afternoon and he'll be available for us after the funeral at midday."

As they drove out through the gates, Sarah shuddered. "Ugh, this place gives me the creeps. It reminds me of the house in the movie 'Psycho', perched on top of the hill, shutters, cobwebs and all."

McNab's mobile rang. Vincent Ng was calling to tell them about his interview with Lola Jones. After McNab finished the phone conversation, he looked at Sarah.

"Right, let's go to Doctor Poulter's office. I believe his practice used to be run by one of the original doctors in the district. Let's hope he's got the records on the Pettys."

The receptionist at Doctor Poulter's office smiled pleasantly at them as they entered. "Can I help you?"

McNab discreetly showed his ID and quietly asked to see Doctor Poulter when he was free.

"Of course, sir, I'll fit you in after he's finished with his current patient," she replied, then went out the back, obviously to advise the doctor that they were waiting.

Ten minutes later, Doctor Poulter ushered them into his office. "Hello Inspector, Sergeant. How can I help you?"

"Doctor, does your surgery have files for Lyle Petty, Celia Petty and Lynda Petty?"

"I have a current file for Lyle Petty Inspector, but I know nothing about either a Celia or a Lynda Petty."

"They wouldn't have been here for over twenty years. Do you keep the previous doctor's files?" asked McNab.

"I'll take you out to Shirley. If anyone knows where to find the records, she will. Mind you, I don't know how much you could use from the files, patient confidentiality and all," replied Poulter.

He called Shirley to come out to the back files office. After introductions, he asked if he could leave. "I've got patients waiting out there. Do you still need me?"

"Not at the moment, Doctor. Thanks for your help," replied McNab.

Twenty minutes later, Shirley had found the two files in question. She called Poulter on the intercom. He saw them within two minutes.

"Sorry Inspector, but ethically, I need to make sure that confidentialities are not going to be breached."

"I understand, Doctor. All we really need to

know is if there is any information, especially in Celia's file, regarding either pregnancy or private adoption."

Poulter opened Celia's file and sifted through the rather large pile of paperwork. "She had a pregnancy test in 1973. There are other papers here that show Doctor Rose organised her trip to Hobart, to stay at a nunnery until the child was born. She died in childbirth. The child, a boy, lived and was to be adopted privately. She used a false name on the birth certificate." Poulter's eyes widened. "Hell. Lyle told me that his sister had died whilst travelling overseas. I didn't know he had another sister named Lynda. I presume, by the look on your face, Inspector, you know where Lynda is?"

"Aye, we do. Does any of the paperwork confirm who adopted the child?"

Doctor Poulter was pale as he confirmed what McNab and Sedgewick already knew. "The adoptive parents are Joan and Roger Wilson. Fancy organising a couple in the same township to adopt the child. There's a birth certificate here, which doesn't give the father's name." Doctor Poulter continued to sift through the large file. "Hold on, there's another letter, from Celia, to Doctor Rose, citing Sir Peter as being the father--Oh, my God!"

"Doctor, can we have a copy of the paperwork that's relevant to the pregnancy, adoption, and fatherhood?" asked McNab.

"Yes, why not. There's been enough harm caused already because of this file's secrets. Yes, of course, I'll give you the copies that you need, Inspector."

Fifteen minutes later, McNab and Sedgewick left the surgery.

"Let's drive to the city office lass. We need to compare notes with Vincent. Besides it's about time I collected my car. Tomorrow, after the funeral, hopefully, we'll all we able to have a long chat with Lyle Petty."

During the fifty-minute drive back to Melbourne, McNab's mind was in a whirl. *So, Sir Peter knew nothing about fathering a second son, until our anonymous left-handed person sent him the evidence. That information made him change his will. We'll never know if Lady Laura knew. If she did, then maybe she intended to kill him. What am I thinking? She was murdered. It's the same handwriting. It's a serial killer!*

Ng met them as soon as they arrived. McNab acknowledged his efforts.

"Well done, lad. Let's look at Celia's photo. Aye, Joe's definitely inherited his mother's eyes."

31

I t was now Tuesday, the fifteenth of January, four days since Sir Peter Percival had been found dead and three days since Lady Laura died. It seemed that the whole township of Sunbury was going to try to see their joint funeral.

The Chapel in the O'Reilly funeral Parlour was small, so Jason Percival had asked only immediate family, close friends and the necessary representatives from the Farmers Co-op, the local council and, of course, the State Parliament.

The funeral director had placed speakers outside the building so that the locals, unable to be inside for the actual service, could listen. It was going to one of those hot, humid days. People had already gathered outside. Some had brought rugs and picnic chairs. They were sitting in the cool shade under the trees in the Village Green, on the other side of the road. McNab surveyed this scene on their arrival and said, "It's like they are having a picnic, instead of attending a funeral."

Andy McNab, Sarah Sedgewick, and Vincent Ng went and stood inside, at the back of the Chapel entrance, so they could watch at a discreet distance. The main interest for the three detectives at this time was to watch each mourner's reactions and body language to see if anyone might reveal their possible involvement in Sir Peter's and Lady Laura's deaths.

It was not a religious service. Instead, Jason had planned to say a few words, followed by Joe Wilson. The State Premier Gordon Jackson had also asked to say a few short official words. Finally, the priest from Salesian College, Sir Peter's old school, was there to consecrate the two remains for burial in the local cemetery that was only a short drive away from the village green.

Ironically, the small cemetery was at the foot of the second biggest hill. It was on the opposite side of the township from where Woodburne stood. Andy McNab had mentally noted this fact before arriving at the Funeral Parlour fifteen minutes before the first official mourners started to enter the chapel.

To McNab, the irony laid in the fact that Woodburne and the winery would be looking down on Sir Peter's gravesite. It was like a display of triumph from the rows of vines, and the bricks and mortar of the house itself, being able to endure long before and after the physical presence of one mere owner. It was a stark reminder to McNab of the brevity in time that humans spent on this ancient planet.

Soft organ music was playing over the loud speakers. At the front of the chapel, the two coffins had been placed side by side. Sir Peter's coffin had a large wreath made out of twisted vines resting on the top, whilst Lady Laura's had a large wreath of red roses. The perfume from the roses permeated the small chapel. McNab whispered into Sarah's ear, "I always start to get claustrophobic in this sort of situation. I'll be glad when all the speeches are finished and we get outside again."

The priest went to the front of the small gathering, ready to start the proceedings. McNab had noted the presence of Jason, Dianne and her husband Fredrico, his parents Pino and Isabella Gambello, Joan and Roger Wilson, Peter Cotti, representing the Co-op, and of course the Premier and the Shadow Treasurer, representing the Opposition.

There was a tall, gaunt man sitting next to Roger Wilson, whom McNab didn't recognise. He made a mental note to speak to this man afterwards. Andy felt that too often things were said on such occasions that were either 'over the top' or often an exaggeration of the truth. The Premier's 'speech' was such an epistle, lasting nearly fifteen, boring minutes.

"This is like a political broadcast," whispered Sarah.

Joe Wilson made the best speech. McNab could

see that he had the qualities of leadership that were innate and sincere. His comments mainly centred on the past, current and future of Woodburne itself and the fact that Sir Peter and Lady Laura were now past custodians. The future lay in the ongoing maintenance of Woodburne as an integral part of the community of Sunbury. When Joe finished his short eulogy, McNab noted the approving nods and smiles from everyone present, including Jason. It was obvious that there was a strong bond between the two young men. Woodburne had been entrusted into safe hands. Sir Peter had done something right, after all.

When McNab and his team stepped outside into the humid day, they felt as though they had literally stepped into another world. Press photographers and television crews jostled for the best positions.

Back into the Circus Ring! McNab thought. He sighed, then smiled at Sarah and Vincent who had been watching him.

"Are you okay?" asked Sarah.

"I'm fine. Let's go and talk to that man who was sitting next to Roger Wilson."

They weaved their way through the mourners. McNab sighted the tall, gaunt stranger, who'd been staring at the coffins going in the two hearses, shuffling away and disappearing into the surrounding crowd.

"Damn it! Don't let him disappear. Vincent, try

and find him," commanded McNab.

"I'll search, too, boss," remarked Sarah.

Vincent and Sarah both returned without the elusive man. McNab managed to reach Roger Wilson, before he got into his car to follow the two hearses.

"Roger, who was that man sitting next to you in the service?" he asked.

Roger Wilson looked surprised, then answered, "Don't you know? That's Sir Peter's elusive hermit neighbour, Lyle Petty."

32

Half an hour later, McNab, Sedgewick and Ng were driving up the long driveway that led to Petty's house. The tall, skeletal figure of Lyle Petty was standing at the door, waiting for them.

"I was expecting you to come and see me earlier than this," he said.

They introduced themselves, showing their ID cards, and then followed Lyle into the cool, front hall of the old, elegant house. It was as if they had stepped back fifty years in time. Everything in the house was old. Lace curtains covered the windows. The furniture was antique with colonial lamps hung from the ceilings. They were ushered into the front lounge room, where they each sat on big, high-backed, padded leather chairs.

"Mr Petty, we've a few questions we'd like to ask," started McNab.

"Start asking, young man," growled Petty.

"We know the payments to your family of Woodburne royalties stopped when Sir Peter took over the Woodburne winery after his father's death. We also know that you tried to contest this," remarked McNab.

"Of course I did, Inspector. I was furious. Graham Percival had honoured the agreement to my father Arthur and when he died, he continued payments to me for six months. That's when my father died. Sir Peter sent me a letter saying that he was stopping the payments. He said it was only an agreement between our grandfathers, Paul Petty and George Percival. He said he wasn't under any legal obligation to continue the payments. I went to my solicitor. We got our claim to a court hearing, but we were defeated. I still think that Sir Peter should've kept paying me. After all, my grandfather set up their winemaking process. I'm glad he's dead."

"You didn't like Sir Peter, did you?" asked Sarah.

"I thought I'd had made that pretty obvious, young lady!"

McNab leaned forward in his chair. He reminded Petty of his legal rights. He then asked if he wanted any legal representation, before they continued their questions. Lyle Petty coughed heavily, turning almost blue in the face. Sarah rushed out and came back, offering him a glass of water.

"Thanks. It's all right--I want to continue. It's time to get things off my chest--one way or another." He sighed, sinking back into his chair.

"Well go on, Inspector. You obviously wish to say something, judging by the look on your face."

"You organised through Doctor Rose, to have Celia's baby adopted by a local childless couple, didn't you?" asked McNab.

"I did? What else am I meant to have done?" He snorted.

"You lied about Celia dying overseas on a holiday. She died in childbirth. The father wasn't noted on the birth certificate, and Celia used a false name. Perhaps that was your idea. But you knew exactly who the father was, didn't you?" continued McNab.

"Go on, Inspector, I'm enjoying your story," smiled Petty.

McNab decided to continue. "You made sure that the Wilson's adopted and reared Joe. That way, you could watch over his progress. You knew something about Joe that Sir Peter didn't know. You used that knowledge to threaten Sir Peter. It worked, but not the way you hoped. You only wanted money from Sir Peter, to keep your vineyard going. Unfortunately for you, Sir Peter, in spite of whom many people thought as self-centred, wanted to make amends to the son that he'd discovered through you. He changed his will. You still didn't have any money. How am I going so far, Mr Petty?"

"Quite a tale, go on." Petty coughed.

"When he refused to give you any money, you plotted his death. You grow herbs, don't you? There's no point in denying this. Vincent has a written statement from your sister, Lynda."

"What's bloody Lynda got to do with this? She walked out of here years ago. She couldn't care less about the vineyard or me. How did you find her? I thought she'd disappeared for good." Petty glared at McNab.

At last, I've hit a raw nerve. "Lynda says she was forced to leave. She was frightened of you. She not only left you, but she changed her name."

"She'd no money. How did she survive?" asked a now curious Petty.

"Oh, she survived Mr Petty. A few years later, she received financial help from a friend, and ex neighbour, called Sir Peter Percival."

Lyle Petty almost choked with a coughing fit again. Five minutes later, the session continued, at his insistence.

"Go on, Inspector, tell the rest of your tale," he croaked.

"You made one final visit to Woodburne, the last evening that Sir Peter was alive. No one was around and, besides, it was easy for you to approach Woodburne through the adjoining fence. You confronted him when he was about to have his evening spa. When he told you that he wasn't going to give you any money, you quietly slipped some of the Poison Hemlock that you were carrying in your pocket into his tumbler of whisky, then left. You only made one mistake that evening. You lost the vial on your way back to your house. You must have had a coughing fit or something and in pulling out your hanky, the vial slipped out and onto the garden bed near the gate. That's where we found it the next day. Poor Lady Laura saw you leaving. She was on her own in the house. Sir Peter was about to have his last evening spa."

Petty coughed some phlegm into his hankie. "This is a fanciful tale, but interesting nevertheless. Go on."

"When she rang you the next day, accusing you of killing her husband, you went to see her. You made sure that you saw her when Joan was busy downstairs, in the back of the house. You slipped Lady Laura some of your deadly mixture in her glass of whisky. Somehow, you convinced her to drink the whisky. Perhaps you said it would help to calm her down. That she was sadly mistaken. I'm sure you'll be able to tell us the exact words in your statement. The result was that she quickly lapsed into unconsciousness as the poison took its hold on her. You cleaned your fingerprints off the glass, then pushed the letter that you'd pre-written which looked remarkably like her writing, into her dying hand. The rest was simple. You only had to quietly leave via the side door, and cross over the side fence, where Joan wouldn't hear or see you."

McNab sat back in his chair and watched Lyle Petty, who coughed again, his hanky covering his mouth.

Petty looked defiantly back at him. "There are no facts to your tale. You've got no proof. It's been an interesting and, as I've already said, a fanciful story, Inspector. I'm not going to confess to you. You won't be able to prove a thing."

McNab stood up, and looked down at the fail, pathetic figure that seemed to shrink back into the chair. He stared straight into the sick eyes. "Oh, don't worry, Mr Petty, we'll find all the proof needed, you can rely on that. You can go to bed tonight and think about the time when Lynda will also eventually inherit what will rightfully be hers, namely your winery!"

McNab thought that Petty was about to choke to death at that moment. After Petty stopped coughing, he cleared his throat and looked at McNab.

"I wish to write a statement. Don't look so pleased, Inspector. It's not a confession. You'll never be able to prove anything. It was a good story, though."

Twenty minutes later, the three detectives left. McNab carried the sheet of paper containing Lyle Petty's statement. Sarah was the first to comment as the car moved down the driveway,

"He's so cocky, boss. How can he even think that he'll get away with murder?"

McNab grinned, held up the statement, and replied, "Och, he won't, lass. As we all witnessed, he wrote it with his left hand! We only need the writing expert to confirm that the same person who wrote Lady Laura's suicide letter wrote this. That'll be as good as a confession."

EPILOGUE
Preening of Feathers

It was Wednesday, the sixteenth of January. Andy McNab was watching the first rays of the sun appearing behind the nearby hills. He'd been up most of the night. He knew that his theory was correct. He was confident that writing experts would confirm Lyle Petty's left-handed statement was the same author who wrote the suicide letter. Only problem was that it might take a little time to get more proof, and they didn't have all that much time. In fact, the D.P.P would probably decide that it wasn't worth the expense of going ahead with the prosecution. After all, everyone now knew that Lyle Petty only had a couple of months to live, at the most. That's unless his cancerous lungs breathed their last tortured breath earlier than the predicted time.

Och, lad, it's finally finished.

He turned around at viewed the portrait of Rhonda. *Aye, lass, I finally have that twinkle in your eyes. You're ready to go on show to the world. You're mum was a finalist, but you're a winner!*

He sighed with satisfaction. He'd spent most of

170

the night prowling up and down in front of the portrait trying to analyse what he'd missed when painting her eyes. Just before dawn appeared, he'd laughed and added one simple stroke of the paintbrush to each eye. The portrait was finally finished. Her ghost had finally left his soul. He had a quick shower, ate breakfast, walked the dogs, and impatiently looked at his watch for the umpteenth time that morning.

Good, I'll phone. She'll be awake now.

"Good morning, Sarah. Yes, I know what the time is--how would you like to have home-made curry dinner tonight with one happy artist?"

THE END

You can find ALL our books up at Amazon at:
https://www.amazon.com/shop/writers_exchange

or on our website at:
http://www.writers-exchange.com

Acknowledgments

This book would not have been possible without the patient support and understanding of my husband, David.

My thanks to Peter and Beverley, for a not only a cosy stay at the Forget-me-not Cottage, Daylesford, but your invaluable insight into herbs and providing me with the perfect lethal poison!

Thank you, Mary, for rekindling my desire to write.

Finally, although set in Sunbury Victoria, the Woodburne Winery, and all the characters exist only in the imagination of the author and bear no relation to places or people in real life.

About the Author

Wendy Laing is one half of the pseudonym or pen name "Dalziel Laing" of Dianne Dalziel and Wendy Laing, the co-authors of *Mirror, Mirror.* She is also a multi-published author in her own right.

In retirement, a writer, with a Teaching Diploma, a Bachelor of Arts Degree with majors in professional Writing (creative writing editing, publishing and Journalism) and Communications (mass media, and gender imaging) with electives in Literary Studies and Sociology, and Master of Arts (project/thesis called: "Severance Packages, A crime/Paranormal Novel and Exegesis focussing on the electronic and Digital publication of Creative Writing".

A "Jill-Of-All-Trades" Teacher, curriculum consultant, travel consultant, International Airline employee in passenger and cargo areas at Melbourne International Airport and city offices, and a Professional Dog Trainer! Wendy's had articles published in *The Sunbury Times* and *The Anthony Warlow International Newsletter.*

Member of the FAW (Fellowship of Australian Writers)
Member of the VWC (Victorian Writers Centre)
Lifetime Alumni of Victoria University
Member of Sister in Crime

Widowed in 2016, Wendy lives in a retirement village with her four pawed family, Vicky, a sooky & loving adopted black Greyhound, whom she has trained and takes to Pet therapy at the local aged care each week - a hobby that she has enjoyed for over 30 years.

Keep track of Wendy's many books on her author page:
http://www.writers-exchange.com/Wendy-Laing.html

If you enjoyed this author's book, then please place a review up at Amazon and any social media sites you frequent!

If you want to read more about books by this author, they are listed on the following pages...

Cock of the Walk
{Murder Mystery}

When Sir Peter Percival, owner of the Woodburne Wine Estate and former member of Parliament, is found dead--Detective Inspector Andy McNab, Detective Sergeant Sarah Sedgewick and Detective Constable Vincent Ng embark upon a baffling investigation--You see, it appears as though everyone has a motive...

This intriguing mystery is set in Wendy's home town of Sunbury, Victoria, Australia, amongst the surrounding vineyards of the Sunbury Wine region.
Publisher Book Page:
http://www.writers-exchange.com/Cock-of-the-Walk.html
Amazon: http://mybook.to/CockOfTheWalk

Jane Doe Mystery Series
{Mystery/Paranormal}

Book 1: Flowers From The Grave

The first in the Inspector Jane Doe adult mystery/paranormal series. Inspector Jane Doe, head of Melbourne Homicide is staying in an isolated cliff top cottage. She's recovering from near fatal head injuries received from a serial killer.

Ryan O'Byrne a stranger on the beach befriends her. Jane's idyllic sojourn turns into a nightmare. Who is sending her flowers with threatening notes attached? Is Ryan truly a ghost? Can she trust Ryan as a friend or is he in fact the serial killer, and she his next victim?

Publisher Book Page:
http://www.writers-exchange.com/Flowers-From-The-Grave.html
Amazon: http://mybook.to/JaneDoe1

Book 2: Severance Packages

Set in the peaceful town of Sunbury, Australia, Jane is once again faced with the prospect of dealing with a serial killer after the grizzly discovery of a dismembered body is made at the local winery...then another at the tip... Who knows how many more 'Severance Packages' will be found?

Publisher Book Page:

http://www.writers-exchange.com/Severance-Packages.html
Amazon: http://mybook.to/SeverancePackages

Book 3: Haunted Hearts

This book is set five years on from the second *Jane Doe* novel, *Severance Packages*.

Jane has been happily married to Oliver Tarrant for five years and they live at Wyndales, Gisborne, and Detective Chief Inspector Steve Ho is now head of the Special Crime Squad.

Jane has just accepted a new job with promotion to Chief Superintendent as head of the Special Cold Case Unit.

Jane's first Cold Case involves an MP's daughter's recent death. He disagrees with the first coroner's verdict of accidental death. The second autopsy reveals that she was murdered. At the same time, Jane's husband, Oliver Tarrant is dealing with a young heart transplant recipient, who is having nightmares of being murdered and Steve Ho is investigating the murder of an eminent heart transplant surgeon, dumped in a local lake.

Eventually, each of these three cases become intermingled. Steve Ho, Oliver Tarrent and Jane are suddenly embroiled together in one of the most haunting cases of their careers.

Jane labels her first cold case, *Haunted Heart*.
Publisher Book Page:

http://www.writers-exchange.com/Haunted-Heart.html
Amazon: http://mybook.to/JaneDoe3

Book 4: Cadavers Cave

Chief Superintendent of the Cold Case Squad, Jane Doe has a formidable list of special, unsolved cases littering her desk. Taking a break is a luxury she doesn't often allow herself. However, during a rare weekend off, she catches a news story involving a dead body wrapped in a plastic shroud. The gruesome discovery was made in the cliffs below the Point Lonsdale Lighthouse--directly near the entrance to the Port Phillip Bay in Victoria, Australia. Rough winter weather combined with unusually heavy, high tides washed away the grave, leaving it partially covered in rocks and seaweed. The coroner estimates that the body had been buried there for at least a year. The last thing Jane needs is another case to hit her already groaning desk, but something eerie took place in Cadavers' Cave and she may be the only one who can solve a mystery equally troubling and tragic.
Publisher Book Page: http://www.writers-exchange.com/Cadavers-Cave.html
Amazon: http://mybook.to/janedoe4cadaver

Mind's Eye-The imagery of

remembered scenes
{Poetry}

A collection of poems written by Wendy over the years, full of images from childhood, family, pets the Australian countryside around her, with a touch of homespun philosophy.
Publisher Book Page:
http://www.writers-exchange.com/Minds-Eye.html
Amazon: http://mybook.to/MindsEye

Mirror, Mirror
with Di Dalziel (writing as Dalziel Laing)
{Murder Mystery}

Mirror, Mirror is a mystery story with two parallel tales. One tale covers a century. It is the history of the Tremble's, Roger's family. It gives a graphic insight into the psyche of 'Roger' the serial killer. The other tale covers the timeframe of a week. It follows Inspector Georgina Borg's pursuit of a serial killer. She has been unable to crack the killer's identity. The murders have been over a period of ten years. She has followed the trail from Sydney to Melbourne. All of the victims have been loners or with distant family and without husband and especially kids. Cate, the last victim, however has a different profile entirely. Borg knows it is the same killer, but why this change of modus operandi? She feels that this will be the killer's downfall.

Borg is convinced that latest victim may complete and solve the serial killers puzzle and reveal his identity. In the meantime Borg's life is an emotional mess. She is unable to commit herself to a permanent relationship with Professor Richard Thompson, but is madly in love with him. During her investigations into the latest killing, Richard becomes a prime suspect!

The two stories reflect upon each other and finally, in a macabre twist, come together. Georgina is then faced with a race against time to try and stop her now 'revealed' killer from leaving her precinct, and perhaps eluding the clutches of the law forever.

Publisher Book Page:
http://www.writers-exchange.com/Mirror-Mirror.html
Amazon: http://mybook.to/MirrorMirror

Sir Henry, the Knight in Space
{Science Fiction/Mid-Grade Reader}

Twin boys accidentally beam up the ghost of Sir Henry de Bohun from the 14th century into their father's spaceship in 3000AD--that's when the fun begins.... They even take a virtual trip back in time and visit Sir Henry's English castle!

Publisher Book Page:
http://www.writers-exchange.com/Sir-Henry-the-Knight-In-Space.html
Amazon: http://mybook.to/SirHenry

Tarmac Tales
By Wendy and Dave Laing

Wendy & Dave Laing have a total of 52 years' experience with Airlines, in Passenger, Cargo, and dealing with Cargo Agents, Passenger Agents, Crew, Catering, and all the less obvious elements that make up the Airline Industry. They have changed names of the characters involved to keep their anonymity.

All the tales are based on fact. People who know them personally will know the names of the airlines for which they worked. This is a collection of experiences, both funny, sad and entertaining, giving you an enlightening behind the scenes peep of this amazing industry!

Publisher Book Page:
http://www.writers-exchange.com/Tarmac-Tales.html
Amazon: http://mybook.to/TarmacTales

Under the Coolabah Tree
{A Collection of Australian Poetry}

Fun, sometimes rowdy and always delightfully full of Australian colour, this collection of Australian Bush poems by Wendy Laing is sure to amuse. Ream 'em aloud if you dare to try an Aussie accent!

Publisher Book Page:
http://www.writers-exchange.com/Under-the-Coolabah-Tree.html

Amazon: http://mybook.to/UnderCoolabah

Printed in Great Britain
by Amazon

39198373R00106